PURITY

A FRIENDS-TO-LOVERS COLLEGE ROMANCE

SKYLER MASON

To Gabrielle, for saving this book the way Jesus saved me

FOREWORD

I was raised in evangelical purity culture and poured my religious trauma into this book. While it has a fairly kind perspective on Christianity as a whole, it does NOT have a kind view of purity culture.

ONE

Livvy

I'LL MISS my silver ring, even though I've grown to resent it. The ocean will swallow it up, just like all the other tiny things that sink. It will be in good company.

I clench it in my fist as the incoming wave steadily grows. I'll wait a moment before I toss it in. There's something satisfying about the symbol of my purity disappearing into crashing water. Just as the wave starts to break, I yank my arm back.

I freeze.

Why is this so hard? It's not as if this ring is my actual virginity. How am I going to have sex by the end of the summer if I can't even toss a piece of metal?

"Livvy," my sister, Vanessa, says, "Why do you need to get rid of your purity ring? What is that going to solve?"

The apprehension in her voice is an echo of my own inner turmoil. Our parents would be devastated if they found out. This ring was a gift from my dad on my thirteenth birthday. It probably means as much to both of them now as it did eight years ago.

Which is exactly why I need to toss it. It's creepy how they fixate on the sex life of their adult daughter, and it's kept me in a box my whole life. I didn't date. I barely even flirted with anyone. It's made me live small even as I dreamed big.

I'm done dreaming.

I'm done fantasizing about someday giving this ring to Cole Walker, along with my purity. For years, I've imagined the day I'd slip off my white dress and give my beautiful best friend all my firsts. It's time to let it go. He'll never be my husband.

He doesn't love me that way, and he never will.

Cole's moving home from college today. He might be driving into town at this very moment, and we'll be closer than we've been in four years.

And I'll be in danger of making him my entire world, just like I did in high school. I was willing to give him anything he needed in the moment he needed it. If he wanted to see me, I'd drop all of my plans. I would have done anything for him, because I loved him so much.

It's time to start living for myself.

"Do it!" Mariana shouts, pulling me out of my head. "Make that ring your bitch!"

I snort. Thank God for Mari. I wouldn't be where I am right now if not for her example. She showed me I can pull away from purity culture and still be a good person. She doesn't even believe in God anymore, yet she's still the same Mariana.

At the sight of an incoming wave, I brace myself, taking a deep breath and lifting my fist. The wave crests and crashes before streaming past my bare feet, sending a chill up my spine.

I can't do it.

Instead, I turn around. Vanessa's posture relaxes a little,

and Mariana lifts both brows. "I hope this doesn't mean you're still planning to save yourself for marriage."

I shake my head sharply. "I'm done with all of that bullshit. Jesus isn't going to stop loving me if I lose my virginity."

Mari claps her hands. "Yes!"

My younger sister's brows pull together, and I look away. I knew she would have a hard time with this, but I'm not going to hide it from her. We've always been each other's confidants, and I'm not letting that change just because my faith has evolved.

Both of them watch me, as if they both know what I'm about to say is monumental.

"I'm losing my virginity by the end of the summer," I say.

Mariana shrieks, and Vanessa's gaze falls to the sand, probably to hide her dismay, and it sends a pang to my chest.

"I even have a deadline." I reach into the bag at my hip and pull out the tin box. Inside is my purity contract, a letter to my future husband, and every prayer journal I've kept since I met Cole five years ago. I pull out my current journal, flip to the last page, and read aloud what I wrote there. "September seventeenth," I say. "UC Santa Barbara's fall quarter starts on the eighteenth, and I refuse to start my senior year of college still a virgin. And it's not just that. There are all kinds of other things I plan to do. All the things I've been too afraid to do. Things I used to think were wrong. I'm going to start going on dates. I'm going to get drunk and go to the bars and make out with random guys."

"Yes!" Mari shouts. "I'm loving this."

"Why?" Vanessa asks. Her tone is gentle, but my heart still clenches at the bewilderment in her eyes.

"Because I'm living an incredibly passive life, and that has to stop, because it's not really living."

"And getting drunk and making out with random guys is really living?"

I stare at her for a moment. "You know that none of this is a condemnation of how you live your life, right?

Her mouth tightens. "I mean, I guess so, but why are you doing these things? You've never had any interest in partying. Why do you think doing it now is going to make you happy?"

"It's not that I've never been interest in partying. I was just afraid. I thought it was all sinful."

"Is it a coincidence that you decided this today," Mari asks, "when a certain person is moving back?"

Goodness, she knows me so well. "No," I say, "I've been having anxiety for a while about what things will be like when he's back in town. Mari, I've spent more time with him over the last few years than I have with you, and he's been living an hour and a half away."

Mari snorts. "That's more Cole's doing than yours. I'm telling you, he's in love with you. When you tell him about all this, he's going to confess that. Mark my words."

"I think so too," Vanessa says.

I shake my head sharply. "He needs me emotionally, but he doesn't want me sexually. That's not the kind of love I want. I want someone who can't keep his hands off me."

"I bet he wouldn't be able to keep his hands off you if he knew you want him." Mari brushes a flyaway strand of dark hair from her face. "In fact, I think you're the reason he's such a fuck-boy. He had to get sex somewhere since he couldn't get it from you."

"No." I shake my head again. "I can't fantasize about that possibility anymore. I can't wait for him to want me. It's toxic. And it's part of the reason I've lived so small."

A wicked smile spreads across Mari's face. "He's going to

absolutely lose his shit when he finds out you're planning on losing your virginity."

I take a deep breath. "I was actually thinking of...asking him to do it for me. Take my virginity, I mean."

Their eyes grow huge, and a wash of hot, tingling shame spreads from my scalp to the tips of my fingers. "I know it sounds crazy since I'm also trying to get over him, but the thing is... I'm so scared to do this, and he's the only person I can think of who would make me feel totally safe."

"Oh my God!" Mariana shouts. "Does this mean you're going to tell him how you feel?"

"Goodness, no!" I shake my head frantically, the thought alone making my throat grow tight. "No way. That would be so humiliating, and it's already going to be hard enough to ask him for this."

Mari smiles cheekily. "Maybe once you tell him you want to have sex, he won't be able to keep his hands off you, just like you've always wanted."

I turn away and look at the water, not wanting her to see how that statement makes hope flutter in my heart. Despite all my efforts to change, I can't seem to squash this wretched hope. Maybe things will change. Maybe he's not attracted to me now because he's never considered me. Maybe he'll find out that he's attracted to me after he touches me.

No. I can't let delusional thoughts like that sway my decision.

"Maybe," I say. "But I'm not going to let his reaction get in the way of my plans. It's time to start living. I'm going to ask Cole at his graduation party. If he says no, I'll have to find someone else. Maybe even Zac—"

Mari burst into laughter. "You are living in a fantasy world if you think Cole will ever let that happen." She turns to Vanessa. "In high school, he—no exaggeration—shoved Zac against a wall for patting Livvy's ass. It was an accidental pat, too. I'm pretty sure he was aiming for her lower back. Even innocent high school Livvy wasn't the least bit creeped out by it, but Cole completely lost his mind. He got written up for it."

Vanessa smiles at me. "He's so protective of you. It's really cute."

"It was cute in high school," I say. "I don't find it cute anymore." Not after years of nothing coming from it. "He's going to have to start keeping his protectiveness in check, because I'm doing this. No matter what. Come on—" I plop down on the soft sand and gesture for them to sit down with me. "I want you to help me come up with things to do. I'm calling it my impurity contract."

"Oh my God," Mari exclaims. "I absolutely love it. Please sign it Olivia Grace Gallo, like you did on your purity contract."

I nod. "I'll make them look as similar as possible."

When Vanessa averts her eyes, something tugs inside of me. Poor thing. She thinks I'm mocking everything she still believes in.

I reach out, grab her hand, and give it a tight squeeze. "Ness, this isn't a critique of our whole religion. Just purity culture. I still love Jesus more than anything."

"I know," she says, but she doesn't sound quite convinced.

I pick up a pen and press it to the top of the page. "Obviously, the first thing I need to do is have my first kiss."

Mari nods. "If you plan on getting drunk, you could knock out two birds with one stone. It's much easier to kiss someone when you're drunk."

I nod slowly. "I think I want to get high too. I always thought if I smoked weed, it would lead to a life of drugs."

"I used to think that too," Mari says. "And I almost lost my mind with paranoia the first time I got high."

Vanessa grimaces. "That doesn't sound fun."

"This isn't about fun," I say. "It's about facing my fears."

Vanessa lowers her gaze to the sand.

"I think you need to add dressing slutty to your contract," Mari says. "Your body shame is probably one of the most toxic things you inherited from purity culture. Especially your hang-up with your boobs. I would kill for your double Ds, and you treat them like they're disgusting."

Just the thought of my chest exposed makes a hot, prickling shame creep over my body, which is exactly why I need to listen to Mari's suggestion.

I nod. "I'll add that."

Five items in total. Now for the final one. The big one. As I start writing down "lose my virginity", I'm halted by my sister's voice.

"I think you should add telling Cole how you feel to your list."

I grow utterly still, and heat creeps along my neck.

Goodness, just thinking about it makes my stomach churn. What if he says he doesn't love me back, that he never could?

I don't think I could bear it.

A strong, assertive woman would tell him how she feels, but I'm not there yet. "I'll think about," I say, "but I think this is good for now." I lift up the list.

1. First kiss
2. Get drunk
3. Smoke weed
4. Dress slutty
5. Have a drunken make-out
6. Lose my virginity

"I don't have to do them in order, but they all need to be

done by September seventeenth, which means if Cole says no, I'll have some work to do, because I'm determined to get this done—"

My phone chimes, and I reach into my pocket. A smile tugs at my lips when I see the name on my screen. "Speak of the devil."

"Cole?" Mari asks.

"Yep," I say as I glance at the text.

Cole: I just finished unpacking, and I'm dying to see you. Do you have time to hang out before the party? Just let me know where you are, and I'll come to you.

Mari glances at my phone and snorts. "Anyone who reads that text would think he's your boyfriend."

My lips tighten. "That's part of the problem. I'm too available for him. I have to start asserting myself more. I was planning on taking my time to get ready so I look really pretty at the party. If I hang out with him now, I won't have time."

I look down at my phone, debating what to text back. My gut instinct is to be overly apologetic, to tell him I'm so sorry I don't have time but promise to be extra early to the party so that we can see each other then.

But I need to start changing the old patterns.

Me: I'm hanging out with Mari and Vanessa, so I won't be able to see you until the party. I have some HUGE news I have to share with you :)

I reread the text and then hit send.

Jesus, help me. There's no going back now.

TWO

Cole

MY PULSE STARTS to pound as I read her text, and a prickle of foreboding runs down my spine. "Huge news"? And not just huge, but "huge" in all caps. What could that possibly be?

This is nothing to worry about. Livvy is thoughtful and sensitive. Often, things that are huge to her are minor to me. She may have had a conversation with a friend that inspired her, or she pushed through her shyness and spoke up more in class.

She has been different these past few weeks in a way I can't quite pinpoint. I've been so busy finishing my last quarter of college, I haven't seen her nearly as much as I usually do, but in our brief interactions, I've sensed a change.

Oh God. Please say she doesn't have a boyfriend. Please say she hasn't met some upright Christian guy that she wants to tell me all about. What if she brings someone to the party tonight to introduce us?

I've always known that once she gets a boyfriend, our relationship will change. Not that she would abandon our friendship. She's too good a person—too steady and strong in her principles—to do that, even if her boyfriend was a jealous prick. But she wouldn't be mine anymore.

Her deepest loyalty would be to him.

Fuck, I hate him already.

"What's wrong?"

I jerk up from my phone to see my mom walking down the pathway from the main house. A breeze brushes over my face, cooling my hot cheeks, and reality settles over me. It's stupid to let myself get so worked up when I don't even know what Livvy has to tell me.

I smile at my mom as she sits down on the porch chair across from mine. "Zac just told me he got a keg of Coors Light," I say, "and I told him to get Stone IPA. I refuse to drink cheap beer now that I'm a college graduate."

She sets her hands primly on her lap. "Well, I don't want any cheap *or* expensive beer on my carpet, so make sure you keep everyone outside tonight. And if anyone needs to crash, they're sleeping in the guesthouse with you. I don't care if you have a lady friend overnight and want privacy. No one is sleeping in the main house this time." She clenches her jaw. "I had to replace the whole living room carpet after your party last summer."

I pretend to wince. "I've actually already told everyone to crash in your knitting room if they get too drunk. The couches are way more comfortable there, and those yarn-bowl things will be perfect if they have to puke."

My mom smiles, rolling her eyes. "If there's even the faintest scent of vomit in my knitting room, you're starting your apartment hunt tomorrow." As if a sudden thought occurs to her, her smile fades, and her dark brows draw together.

"Honey, I do have to talk to you about something. I wish I could save it until after all of your graduation festivities are over, but it can't wait. I've already waited too long to tell you."

"Okay." I can't keep the apprehension out of my voice.

She opens her mouth and closes it. "I asked your dad for a divorce last week."

The words hit me like a meteor. My pulse starts to pound in my throat. I push myself up from my seat and walk to the edge of the patio. The outer edge of my vision blurs for a moment.

Why am I so surprised when I've been waiting for this? My dad has been an utter shit husband for as long as I can remember, and it's not like it's going to affect me much. I only plan to live in the guesthouse until I find my own place.

What is this strange tingling over my skin? Why do I feel like I'm being swept back in time to that horrible night when I walked in on my dad with that woman, and the whole world shifted?

"Your dad didn't take it well." Her words come in as if from a distance. "I'm not sure if he even fully accepts that I'm going to do it. I asked him to move out as soon as he can, but he looks like he's going to drag his feet."

Finally coming back to myself, I huff. "That sounds about right, since he treats you like your whole life revolves around his."

"Well, I don't know about that, but he's having a hard time. I think getting a divorce lawyer will be a good reality check for him. I'm planning on starting my search tomorrow."

I turn around to face her. "Mom." I try to say the word firmly, but my voice quivers. I clear my throat to keep it from shaking. "Let me find you a good divorce lawyer. That's going to be crucial. I'll start looking—"

"Absolutely not. I'm not letting my *son* find a divorce

lawyer for me. That's not why I told you. I wanted you to have time to process it all before you start at Walker Industries—"

"Don't worry about me. I'll feel better if you let me take care of this. Zac's dad is a lawyer, and he knows all the best lawyers in Santa Barbara—"

"No, Cole." She stares at me for a moment before her hard expression softens. "I love that you're looking out for me, but I need to navigate this process myself. If I'm going to live on my own and take care of myself without your dad's help, this is where it starts."

I want to protest, but I only nod. I know that she's right, but it doesn't stop this itching anxiety crawling over my skin. She may not find the right lawyer. The fact that she hasn't even started looking for one attests to that, especially since she asked my dad for a divorce a week ago. She's so vulnerable after years of having all of her basic needs taken care of by him. That's probably why she stayed with him, even after years and years of heartache.

"Okay, just make sure you find someone ruthless. Someone who will take him for all he's got."

Her posture straightens. "Well, since that would affect the company, and therefore you and your brother and sister, I won't be doing that."

Of course she won't. She's made it abundantly clear to me over the years how important it is to her that I take over Walker Industries someday, and given what she's had to put up with from my dad, it's the least I can do for her. Even though I dread having to work for him.

"Marriages are complicated," she says. "Divorce is never just one person's fault."

I look away, my jaw clenching. Arguing with her will lead to a conversation I don't want to have—to something she and I have only really discussed in code. The one time I tried to tell her the details of my dad's infidelity, she didn't want to hear it. She said she already knew.

God, how fucking sad.

I wish she knew her value. I wish she knew that she deserves to clean him out for everything he's worth after what he's put her through.

"Honey."

When I glance up, my mom's brows are furrowed. "Do you want to talk about what you're feeling? I can tell that you're really upset."

"I'm fine." The words are clipped.

"Okay." Her voice is resigned. "I'll give you your privacy. Don't worry about setting up for the party. I already enlisted Mason to put out more lawn furniture. He doesn't know anything yet about the divorce. I'm still trying to figure out how to tell him and Maddy. But I want you to take some time to yourself, okay? Relax before your party."

I swallow to ease the tightness in my throat. "I'm honestly fine, Mom. It's a long time coming, and I'm happy for you."

She stares at me for a moment. "Well, if you're ever not fine, just know you can talk to me about it."

She walks away, and the world around me blurs. It's really happening. They're divorcing, and the world is shifting under my feet, just like it did years ago. Why am I like this? Why can't I just be strong for my mom?

Fuck, there's only one person who can make me feel anchored again.

I'll tell Livvy the whole story, just like I always do when something is troubling me. She'll stare at me with those soft brown eyes and that little furrow on her brow. She'll say, "Oh Cole, I'm so sorry," in that sweet, melodic voice and shyly ask if it would weird me out if she prayed for me. I'll fight a smile and tell her no, that just because I'm not religious doesn't mean I'm ruling out the possibility that God exists.

She'll set her hand on my shoulder, which will send electricity down my arm. She'll close her eyes and mouth words to herself—careful not to say them aloud because she probably doesn't want to scare me with the strange jargon. And I'll just watch her, relishing her closeness and warmth, absorbing all of her compassion and kindness by proximity.

In a perfect world, I could hold her afterward—pull her into my arms and press her soft body against mine. I'd trail my lips along her neck before taking a little bite of her pretty skin. Then I'd bury myself inside her and—

Fuck.

What am I doing?

The divorce must be throwing me off-kilter. These old fantasies only seem to surface when I'm at my most vulnerable. No matter how much they might provide a balm to my shitty mood, I can't indulge them. I'll never have that part of her, and even if I could, I wouldn't want it. What I have with her is already perfect as it is.

Passion always fades eventually, but my friendship with Livvy is lifelong. I won't do anything to jeopardize it.

I'll want to kill any boyfriend she introduces me to, if that's what she's going to do tonight—mostly out of jealousy—but I'll have to keep any animosity under the surface. She can never know.

This lingering attraction to her has never done me any good. I have to keep it in check.

THREE

Livvy

"ARE YOU NERVOUS?" Mari asks as we park on the stone-tile drive of Cole's parents' house.

I sigh. "I'm so nervous I feel like I have to pee, and I just peed right before we left."

She chuckles as she unbuckles her seatbelt. "I'm pretty sure Cole is going to be as giddy as a kid on Christmas morning when you ask him, but I understand. It's scary when you don't know exactly how he feels." She turns to me, her expression growing stern. "But you're not going to pine over him if he says no. Be thankful he's a hot guy, and hot guys have hot friends. If things go bad tonight, I already have a plan. I'm going to get you nice and drunk, and I'll have your first make-out partner lined up and ready to go in no time."

I smile sadly. "That's sweet of you."

But pointless. If Cole says no, I'll be too dejected for anything other than going home and writing about it in my journal. I'll have to start my hunt for someone else after I've had some time to recover.

When she steps out of the car, I take a deep, calming breath before following her. We walk around the side of the house until we spot a group of people at the edge of the property, near Cole's guesthouse.

"I'm going to go find us a drink," Mari says before turning toward the keg on the patio.

I glance around, looking for Cole. Tall as he is, it takes me only a moment before I spot him. He's standing near the Koi pond with a red cup in his hand and is surrounded by a few girls I vaguely remember from high school. One of them looks like she's in the middle of telling a story. She gestures wildly while she talks, and Cole's eyes are fixed on her face. Riveted.

Goodness, she's so pretty. They always are. Pretty and outgoing, just like him.

I take a deep breath. I can do this. I don't have to be the textbook shy girl who stands silently in a group conversation, patiently waiting for a turn to talk that will never come—that she'll never take, even if it does.

I can be bold.

Boldness is a choice, not a feeling.

I walk steadily in his direction, trying to make my strides large and confident. As if sensing my presence, he looks in my direction. His eyes widen for a moment before his ruggedly handsome face melts into an almost boyish smile. Goodness, he's so beautiful, with his broad shoulders and square jaw and those kind brown eyes. He's everything I was taught to want in a husband—strong and confident on the outside, but soft and caring within.

That's where the delusion started. I'd been so sure that I couldn't love him so much, that he couldn't be the embodiment of all my husband fantasies, if God weren't trying to tell me we were meant to be.

It's sad.

So sad.

As soon as I get close, he opens his arms wide. I quicken my steps and am startled when he pulls me into a tight embrace. He hums as his mouth grazes my head.

Wow. This is different. He rarely hugs me like this, and it tugs at that familiar ache in my belly.

"I missed you," he whispers.

"I missed you too."

"Never again. We're never doing long distance ever again." He squeezes me so tightly that I can't take a breath for a moment. Goodness, he's in a strange mood.

When he finally lets me go, I smile up at him. "I don't know if LA to Santa Barbara could really be called a long distance." *Because we're not in a relationship,* I add silently.

"Well, it was too long for me." He sets his hand on my shoulder before turning to the two girls. "Do you guys remember my best friend, Livvy? She was a year behind us at San Marcos."

One of the girls only nods, but the vivacious one who was telling a story earlier grins mischievously at me before looking at Cole. "I remember you punching Zac in the face for hugging Livvy, and then getting suspended from the baseball team for it."

An adorable little smile tugs at Cole's lips. "Yeah, I was a little overprotective of her, but that particular story gets wilder every year since we graduated. I swear by our ten-year reunion, it'll be that I beat him within an inch of his life and went to jail for it. I didn't even punch him. I shoved him a little bit."

"Not a little bit," I say. "You shoved him really hard."

He narrows his eyes playfully on my face before turning to

the other two. "For the record, it was much more than a hug. He was getting handsy with her, and she didn't like it. I was really just trying to push him away, and I didn't mean to do it that hard."

"Zac wasn't being that handsy," I say to the girls and then grin saucily at Cole. When his eyes widen, my stomach flutters.

I think I'm actually flirting, and in front of a group of people!

"I believe her side of the story, Cole," the vivacious girl says.

He shakes his head. "Your loyalty goes out the window if someone gets hurt." He turns to the girls. "She only gets mad at me when I hurt someone, even if it's only their feelings. I remember one time she wouldn't talk to me for two days straight because she thought I'd hurt Noah's feelings, and she'd never even talked to the guy. I had to send this long text apology to him, which was awkward as fuck, but that was the only way she'd talk to me again, and—" he turns to me, and his eyes grow hooded, "—how did Noah respond to my apology, Livvy?"

I smile sheepishly. "He said he didn't have any idea what you were talking about."

"Yep, that's right. You wouldn't talk to me for two days over imaginary hurt feelings."

I purse my lips. "I still think he was too embarrassed to admit he was hurt. I saw the look on his face when you teased him."

His eyes widen, but his grin stays fixed. "I can't believe you. You will die on this hill. Almost five years later, you're still protecting a guy you don't even know for something he wasn't even upset about."

"Sensitive people don't always say what they feel. I almost

never speak up for myself when someone hurts me. For some reason, it's easier to speak up for other people."

Cole's expression softens. "That's why so many people trust you even when they aren't super close to you. They know you'll have their back no matter what. You're an angel."

Something about the way he says "angel" makes warmth wash over my whole body. He often calls me an angel, and I've never particularly liked it. It usually makes me feel like even more of a boring goody-goody than I know I am, but the way he said it this time...with heat and darkness in his voice. Goodness, he really is in a strange mood.

Something happened today. He's upset, and he needs affection.

Cole looks beyond my shoulder. "I think we bored them with our reminiscing."

My head darts to the side, and I see the two girls have drifted slightly away from us and are now engaged in their own conversation.

"Reminiscing isn't really fun unless you're a part of it," I say.

"It's okay. I really just want to hang out with you anyway."

My stomach flutters. I just want to hang out with him too. I'm never more happy than when it's just the two of us.

"Is something going on?" I ask. "You seem kind of down."

His face falls, and he lifts his red cup to his lips. "Just shit with my parents, as usual."

I nod slowly. "Is it about your new job? That you have to work for your dad soon, I mean?"

"We can talk about it later. I want to hear your news fir—"

"Livvy!"

I jerk in response to Mariana's voice. She walks in our direction with a guy at her side, and I narrow my gaze on his face. He looks familiar. It's only when he's a few feet away that I recognize him as an old church friend.

"Cole," Mariana calls out as she reaches us. "How did I not know before now that you're friends with Travis? Livvy and I grew up with him. He went to our church."

Cole's brows draw together, and something that looks like panic fills his eyes. His head snaps in my direction. "Did you come here with Travis?"

I frown. "No..."

"No, I just ran into him," Mari says.

I notice Cole's shoulders soften at that.

What is going on?

Mari turns to me, pulling Travis's arm. "Livvy, I think there's a lot of potential here." She lowers her voice so only I can hear her and adds, "He's a Christian who fucks."

I shoot wide eyes at her even as a smile rises to my lips. "Mari!" I admonish before glancing at Travis, who's smiling at me.

"She told me you've never gotten drunk before," he says, "and you're looking to have a drunken make-out session. I just want you to know that I'm here for you." His smile grows as he reaches out his hand for me to shake.

I reluctantly take it, resisting the urge to laugh at Mari's tactics. I'm pretty sure this is more of an attempt to rattle Cole than to find me someone to kiss.

"What are you talking about?" Cole asks, his voice much firmer than it was before.

Mari shoots me a knowing smile before glancing at Cole. "Has she told you her news yet?"

"No, she hasn't." His eyes are hard when he turns to me. "Do you want to go somewhere private so we can talk?"

It sounds like much more of a command than a question. I

shoot Mari an exasperated look, and she gives me a small, cheeky smile back.

"Yeah, let's go," I say.

"Good luck," Mari mouths as Cole and I start walking in the direction of the guesthouse.

"Is she wasted?" Cole asks. "Why would she tell Travis you want to have a drunken make-out session?"

I exhale. "I'll tell you when we get inside."

He halts in his tracks and turns around, his tall form hovering over me. "So there's some truth to it? What is going on?"

The alarm has returned to his voice, and it softens something inside my chest. His tone reminds me of my sister today on the beach. It's disorienting when the people we love change, even when those changes don't directly affect us.

Still, if he's this freaked out over some drunken kissing, how is he going to react when I ask him to take my virginity?

I take a deep breath. "You know how I've been struggling with some aspects of my faith?"

"Yeah..." He doesn't sound any less alarmed.

"Well, the bulk of it is really just the purity part. I don't think it's healthy for me. I've come to see the word 'pure' as loaded and toxic. It implies that I'm tainted if I explore my sexuality."

"I've always kind of thought that, but—" He closes his mouth and averts his gaze from mine. "Sorry, I shouldn't say things like that."

A warm smile rises to my lips. He's always been so gracious about my religion, even the more extreme aspects it. Before I met him, I thought atheists were devil worshippers. The respect he's showed for my faith marvels me.

"It's okay to agree with me," I say. "It doesn't mean you don't respect my religion."

He nods slowly, his eyes growing absent as he glances around the lawn. "What does this mean? Are you really going to...get drunk and make out with someone?"

"It's more than that. I have a whole plan for this summer. I have so much fear associated with all of the things that normal college students do, like going to parties and kissing boys. I've decided I need to attack it head-on. I actually wrote a list." It takes my fingers only a moment to find the crisp paper inside my purse. "Mari and Vanessa helped me with it."

As I unfold the paper, his expression grows even more bewildered, but I press on. "These are all the things I plan to do by the end of the summer. I even set a deadline—September seventeenth. It's the day before I start my senior year."

I hand him the list so that I can let it do the explaining for me and spare me the embarrassment of having to say the last one aloud. Cole's brows draw together as he takes it from my hand. His gaze darts over the paper, and my throat grows tight. What is he going to say when he sees the last item? When his eyes nearly pop out of his skill, my stomach churns.

Here we go.

"Livvy, what is this?" His voice is quiet and oddly empty.

"I'm calling it my impurity contract."

His chest rises and falls rapidly, and his nostrils flare. He opens his mouth and closes it. He shuts his eyes for a moment and takes a deep breath, as if collecting himself. When he speaks again, his voice is much gentler. "I know it must be hard being so sheltered. Having your first kiss and getting drunk seem completely reasonable, but losing your virginity? In three months?"

"It probably seems drastic to you—"

"Drastic? It's fucking insane! How are you going from your first kiss to losing your virginity in three months? You don't even have a boyfriend!"

Heat washes over my face and my chest. "You have sex all the time, and you don't want to be in a relationship at all."

He takes another deep breath, lifts both hands, and runs his fingers through his dark hair. "That's different."

He's clearly upset, so I won't call him out on the unfairness of the double standard. I won't tell him how even though his protectiveness warms me, it sometimes makes me feel like a child. Instead, I stand in silence, giving him a moment to calm down.

"How did this happen?" he eventually asks. "You've been adamant about saving yourself for marriage for as long as I can remember."

I keep my voice very soft. "A lot of my adamancy came from fear, I think. Fear of being tainted, of disappointing God and my future husband. But I don't think I can marry a man who only wants me if I'm pure, even if he was raised the way I was."

He nods slowly.

"I want to live a full life," I say. "I don't want to deprive myself of experiences out of fear. I'm about to start my last year of college, and I want to live like every other college student. Like you and Zac and Mari do."

"So is this like Rum-something? I can't remember what it's called. The thing Amish people do?"

"Um..." My brow knits. "Do you mean Rumspringa?" I clench my teeth to keep from smiling, not wanting to shame him for lumping all Christian religions together. How would I expect an atheist to understand the nuances? "That's not something evangelicals do."

"I know, but is it similar? Like, are you planning on getting all of this out of your system before you settle back into your religion?"

"No, it's not like that at all. My faith is evolving. I'm still a Christian, just a different kind than I was raised to be."

"Okay, but why are you doing it like this?" He lifts my contract. "Why not just wait until you find a guy you really like. A Christian guy who's in the same place as you. Someone who believes in God but doesn't want to wait until marriage either. Then you can get to know each other and go through these things at a normal pace."

"No, that won't work. I've already missed out on so much of college life, and I refuse to start my senior year still a virgin. It's time to face my fears. If I take it slow, I'll never do it. I'll end up waiting until I'm married to have sex, not because I want to, but because it's the easiest route." I point to the paper in his hand. "These things shouldn't be scary or shameful, but they are to me, and with that fear comes all this baggage. Cole, I can't even masturbate without feeling guilty afterward."

His gaze snaps to my face, and his eyes grow wide. Even in the dusk, I can make out the brush of pink over his cheekbones.

I lower my gaze to the lawn. "Sorry if that makes you uncomfortable."

"No, it's okay." His voice has a raspy quality to it, and it makes me want to shrink inside myself. Jesus, help me, how am I going to ask him to take my virginity when he gets this awkward over hearing me say I masturbate.

"Livvy." His tone is as firm as it's been since we started this conversation. "This isn't the way."

My gaze snaps up. "What do you mean?

"I mean, doing all this before mid-September is a bad idea. You need to take it much, *much* slower." He crosses his arms over his chest and stares down at me with hard dark eyes. "I won't stand by and let you do something I know is going to make you miserable."

My jaw clenches. I shouldn't be upset. I knew Cole would

do this at some point. He has a commanding disposition in general, but he's especially bossy with me. I can't blame him.

I'm an easy target.

I hate what his bossiness stirs within me. I hate that my first instinct is to submit to him. With effort, I lift my chin. "Why is that for you to decide? Why isn't it enough for me to say this is right for me?"

His hard expression softens before he shuts his eyes. "I just don't want you to get hurt."

I set my hand on his arm. "I appreciate that you're looking out for me, but I need you to trust me."

His eyes pop open. "How is this right for you when you're so shy? I intentionally kept this party really small—" he gestures over my shoulder, "—because I didn't want you to be overwhelmed. How are you going to lose your virginity to a guy you barely know?"

Heat breaks out along my neck. It's time to ask him, even if I'm dreading his response. "I was actually thinking of asking someone I know really well."

His eyes widen in a look that could almost be described as horror, and then he looks away from me. "You mean you have someone in mind already?"

"Yeah." My voice is faint.

The bulge on his throat rises and falls unsteadily. "Someone from your old church?"

"No."

Jesus, help me. It's now or never.

"Cole, I'm talking about you."

FOUR

Cole

A HEAVINESS SETTLES over my body, hushing the world around me. For a moment, there's only her. Those soft brown eyes that somehow had the power to make me feel safe and loved even when I hardly knew her. That plump pink mouth that I've had to train myself to never look at too long. I'm brought back to those heady moments years ago when I thought this angel could actually be mine.

How is this happening? How did everything shift in the span of five minutes?

For so long, she's been out of reach. I had to bury the idea we could be together and force myself never to revisit it, or else our friendship would never work. You can't pine for someone who can never truly be yours, not if you want them in your life long term.

I don't just want her, I *need* her.

But in a sexual way, she's not for me. She's a Christian, and

she'd only ever be with another Christian, and not the kind
who simply believes in God and goes to church every Sunday,
but someone whose faith colors every aspect of their life. The
type of Christian I couldn't pretend to be even if I wanted to.

I did try, long ago.

As much as this difference between us felt like a tragedy at
one time, it's exactly as it should be. If she were willing to be
with an atheist, she'd be gone by now. I would have snatched
her up the minute I saw her. Our relationship would have been
heaven at first, steady happiness for a while, and then it would
have gone sour, like all relationships inevitably do. She'd be
only a memory right now, instead of the most precious and
dependable thing in my life.

I can't do this.

I *cannot* do this.

But, oh God, why does it have to be so hard to say no? I've
never been able to fully put out that flicker of need for her,
despite all my efforts, and now it's consuming my whole body
like a wildfire.

I want to pull her to the ground, shove myself inside her,
and never come out again.

"Livvy," I say, only able to manage a whisper.

When she holds up a hand, I wince. She's going to try to
convince me.

"Just hear me out before you say no."

I sigh, shutting my eyes tightly. God, I need a moment. I'm
too raw right now. "Okay."

"I know it's probably hard for you to see me in a sexual
way."

If I wasn't so riled up, I would laugh. What would she think
if she knew the depravity of my thoughts? From the moment
she first told me about her bizarre purity pledge, I've fantasized
about breaking it.

She'd be terrified.

"I know you're probably thinking it would ruin our friendship or make things awkward between us, but I really don't think it will. Not if we approach it methodically. This isn't strictly about sex. This is about you helping me do something that I'm afraid of. You're the best person to do it, because I trust you so much."

Fuck. How am I going to tell her no when she phrases it like that? I love having her unflinching trust. I've worked hard over the years to show her I'm worthy of it.

"Cole, I know you're freaking out, but listen. Think about this like..." Her gaze grows unfocused. "It's like I'm afraid of heights, so I want to get over my fear by going on a rollercoaster, but the only way I could get myself to do that is if my best friend, who makes me feel safe, goes on it with me. It's not about sex, it's about helping me, and you're the perfect person to do it, because you have sex all the time. You're the type of person who's comfortable having sex with people you aren't—"

"You don't know what type of person I am!" I can't stop myself from raising my voice. "You don't know anything about sex. You don't know what I'll be like. You don't even know what *you'll* be like. You know nothing."

When she flinches, I hate myself. Goddamn it, temptation is stretching my composure thin. I take a deep breath and release it slowly. My voice is much gentler when I speak again. "You don't know how you'll feel, because you have no experience. People have a certain..." I shut my eyes for a moment, searching for the right word. Fuck, it's so hard to talk about this stuff with her when she's so damned innocent. "People have a certain style. When they have sex, I mean. Not everyone likes the same things. Just based on what I know about you, I don't think you and I would like the same things, and even if I tried to do it how you'll probably like it, people can get kind of... You can lose yourself in the moment. Do you have any idea what I'm trying to say?"

Her expression grows a little exasperated. "I'm not completely ignorant. I told you I masturbate, and my fantasies can sometimes get a little...wild when I'm really getting into it—"

"Okay, um..." I lift a hand while using the other to adjust the waistband of my jeans as discreetly as possible. "Can we just stick the issue?"

Her brow furrows. "How was I not talking about the issue?"

"I mean, let's just talk about you and me, and what this would mean for us."

"Why do you get so awkward whenever I try to talk about anything sexual? Do you find me repulsive?"

I shut my eyes tightly, inwardly begging my racing pulse to slow down. Fucking Jesus Christ, what did I do to deserve this? "Of course not," I rasp. "You're a beautiful girl."

"Then why is it so hard for you to imagine having sex with me?"

It's not. Oh God, it's not at all. The only hard thing about it is in my pants, and it's about to make me give in if she doesn't stop trying to convince me. I have to stop this now.

"Because I'm worried it might change things between us," I burst out. "I'm worried that I'll scare you, and you'll never be able to see me the same way again."

"Why do you get to decide what will scare me?" She's as close to yelling as I've ever seen her. "Why does your sexual experience make you more of an expert on how I would feel than I am?"

I exhale heavily, lowering my gaze to the grass. "It doesn't. The truth is, neither of us know how things would change if we do this, and forgive me if I don't want to be your science experiment."

I ought to tell her the real reason—the true fear. *I'm afraid you'll fall in love with me. I'm afraid I'll fall in love with you. Once that happens, we'll be on a path toward destruction.* She could never understand. She's too naive to realize that romantic love is really just intense sexual desire in disguise. And desire always fades.

When the warmth of her hand touches my arm, my stomach jolts.

God, her touch feels so good. Why does it have to feel so good? Why does the only person in the world who makes me feel safe and happy also have to ignite me like this?

"I don't want you to feel that way," she says. "That makes it sound like I'm using you."

I set my hand on top of hers, relishing her warmth for one brief moment before I let it go. "I know you're not using me, and I want to be able to help you with all of this, but it's a huge deal. It's not something I can just decide on without thinking about it."

"I don't want you to rush it. Take all the time you need to think about it."

I grunt. Somehow, I've gone from a definitive "no" to thinking about it, all in the span of a few minutes.

Oh God, how am I going to resist her?

I don't think she should be doing any of this in the first place. She's not ready. Her idiot parents sheltered her to the point of ignorance. Mari and I have tried to fill in the gaps, but it's been hard when Livvy gets so nervous and clammed up when we get too explicit about some of our own sexual experiences.

She's so damned vulnerable. She shouldn't be getting drunk

and making out with strange guys, because she never learned how to protect herself.

I need to protect her.

"Look," I say. "All I can do right now is promise to help you with your impurity contract. I'll be there when you get drunk and high. I'll stay sober to make sure you're safe. If you want to have a drunken make-out session..." I grit my teeth. "I can be nearby in case the guy tries something with you, something that makes you uncomfortable."

When she looks like she's fighting a smile, I frown. "What?"

"That's fine as long as you don't scare him away."

"I wouldn't do that."

Her smile grows. "You have done it in the past."

"Only because I knew you didn't want it."

"You've scared away guys for just talking to me."

My cheeks grow hot. "They weren't Christians. Until now, you didn't want any attention from guys who weren't Christians."

"I never said that."

"Well, you've told me plenty of other things, and I read between the lines. I didn't want you to get any unwanted attention."

"I know." She smiles warmly. "You're such a caring friend. Thank you for helping me with my contract, even if you don't agree with it."

For a moment, our gazes hold. God, she's so beautiful. So damned beautiful and sweet. I could keep myself in check and give her the kind of first time she wants. I could light candles, kiss her softly, push into her slowly and—

No.

I don't want vanilla sex with her, and I could never be satisfied with only a small slice of heaven. I'm too greedy for her touch after years of deprivation. I want to lick her for hours, pulling away just before she comes. I want to spank her for all the times she made me hard against my will, like she did a moment ago. And when she's ready to be a good girl, I'll slam into her tightness and tell her that I own her now.

Fuck.

I can't let myself imagine it. This is how I used to think years ago, and it's dangerous.

"Can we start tomorrow?" she asks.

"Tomorrow?" My voice is a rasp.

Her brow furrows. "With my contract. Mari and I are going shopping to buy me some cute outfits. You know, so I can dress *slutty*." When she says the last word in an almost whispered voice, I almost laugh. She's so sheltered, she still can barely even say sex-related words. How does she think she's going to lose her virginity in three months?

She's probably not really going to do it. She didn't even want to spend the night in my apartment that time she came down with a fever during her visit to LA. Even with a 101 temperature, she still tried to insist on making the hour and a half drive home at the end of the day. If I hadn't called her parents and gotten them on my side, she probably would have. That was barely over a year ago.

She couldn't have changed this much in a year. I'm probably freaking out for nothing.

"And then we're planning on going out to the bars tomorrow night," she says. "Can you come? I'm hoping if I get drunk, I'll be able to loosen up enough to start flirting and maybe even make out with a guy."

When her face lights up, I want to hit something. Oh God, I don't like this. I don't even like hearing her say it.

"I can do that." I manage a small smile, but then I look at her sternly. "I'll be ordering all your drinks and keeping an eye on them all night. And you won't be going off anywhere by yourself. Not your first time drinking."

Her lips form a little mocking pout. "Yes, Daddy."

I snort. That's yet another innocent thing she does. She says things that are completely innocuous to her but highly sexual to a filthy bastard like me. Without fail, it makes my dick twitch.

"Do you think you can come help me pick out a dress, too?" she asks. "I know Mari is going to try to get me to show off my whole chest no matter what, because she's really trying to get me out of my shell, and I feel like you might be a good foil for her."

I frown. "How so?"

"Well, I think you'll tell me if a dress is too much. If it shows off way more of my boobs than most girls do when they go out."

I clench my jaw. "You want me to look at dresses and tell you if they show off too much of your boobs?"

Her expression shutters. "I mean, if that's too awkward for you—"

"No, no," I interrupt. "It's not awkward. I'm happy to do it."

A half-truth. Unfortunately, the part of me that's happy to do it might also compel me to give her an impulsive, "Yes, I'll have sex with you," at the sight of those big, beautiful, and probably soft—

Fuck, I'm doing it again.

When I lift my gaze, she's staring up at me probingly.

"What?" I ask.

"I have one more thing to ask you." She sucks in both lips before letting them out of her mouth slowly. "Would it be too weird for you to give me my first kiss?"

The question is soft and timid, and it makes me hot everywhere. Why am I being tortured like this?

Still, it's just one kiss, and it's her first. A primitive part of me wants to have it, even if I can never have anything else. Given her inexperience, it probably won't even be much of a kiss. Just a peck.

I can handle a peck.

I smile warmly at her. "Sure."

When she pouts her lips slightly, a prickle of foreboding spreads over my skin. Just looking at that full mouth makes me want to pull her to the ground.

I take a deep, shaky breath before stepping forward. She's so tiny that I have to lower my head quite a bit to bring my face close to hers. When our lips are inches apart, I set my hand gently on her cheek and trail it down.

That's a mistake.

The warmth of her skin sends an electrical charge into my gut and propels me to crash my mouth against hers. She doesn't kiss me back right away, but she parts her lips, and, oh God, they're so soft. As soft and sweet as a marshmallow. I nibble at them a few times before slipping my tongue inside her mouth.

Her tongue is heaven against mine, even when she doesn't move it. *You need to stop now. You'll lose yourself if you don't.* I'm just about to force myself to pull away when she ignites.

She kisses me back, her tongue massaging mine. She doesn't know what she's doing. This is far too aggressive for a first kiss, probably because she's trying to do what she thinks is right. Jesus Christ, I'm going to explode. I grip her shoulders and pull her small, plump body against mine, relishing all that delicious softness.

When she releases a quiet little hum, I grind my hips against her. Oh God, I want to plunder her. I want to shove her against that tree behind us, yank down her pants, and—

Fuck.

I grip her shoulders and shove her away, turning around while I catch my breath. When I lift a hand to run it through my hair, my gaze is drawn to my fingers.

I'm shaking.

I'm actually shaking...from a kiss.

When I turn around, her lips are wet and pink, and the sight of them sends a fire into my belly. God, I need to get away from her soon, before I'm compelled to do it again.

"That was a really good kiss," she says with a sweet little smile.

The sight of her slightly disheveled hair and big trusting brown eyes makes me want to burst out of my skin. Why does she have to be so tempting?

I can't do this. Not if I want her in my life long term. Not if I want her forever.

I have to resist her.

FIVE

Livvy

"HOW DID IT GO?" Mari asks on the drive home. Out of the corner of my eye, I see her wide grin. She must be able to sense my excitement.

That kiss. My goodness, that kiss.

"I'll tell you everything when we get to my house. If my sister is still up, I want to be able to tell her too."

"I knew it! It's good news."

I smile. "Maybe."

"Shit!" Mari glances out the passenger window. "We're in your neighborhood. Do I smell like alcohol?"

Her warm breath tickles my face, and I wrinkle my nose. "A little bit, but don't worry. My parents are probably asleep. And they won't say anything even if they can tell you're drunk."

She snorts. "Not to me, but you know our dads talk. Have you heard about their Christian bro dates? Apparently, they get together once a month to play tennis, get lunch at California Pizza Kitchen—how like our dads is that?—and then pray for me. In that order. Every time. My mom very passive aggressively told me all about it the other day."

A sad smile rises to my lips. I didn't know that was what my dad and Hector did when they hung out, but it sounds very like them. "They're praying for something they don't understand."

"I know, but it's annoying, and it's only because my parents know I party and *suspect* I've had sex before. Can you imagine what they would do if they found out I'm an atheist?"

I purse my lips to the side. "Have you ever thought about telling them?"

She snorts. "Fuck, no. It'll be like sophomore year when my mom found my vibrator. She'll invite all my tias over, and they'll have another hour long prayer session."

A giggle bursts from my chest. "I forgot about that."

"My parents have no chill, so there's no point in telling them anything. I don't mind going to church with them every once in a while. Have you seen the new First Covenant worship leader?"

I shake my head. "He started after I left. Vanessa told me he's hot."

"Oh my God, Livvy. Hot does not do him justice. I want to corrupt him. Fantasizing about it is the only thing that gets me through the sermon."

I giggle. "I think you could, too. He's probably never met a woman who owns her sexuality like you do. He'd be mesmerized."

"Or he'd be terrified. My parents would *definitely* be terrified to know I think about things like this. They'd murder me."

"They think it's a sin just having normal sexual thoughts. Speaking of which..." I sigh heavily as I pull into my driveway. "I'm so nervous to tell my parents I'm done with purity culture.

I'm dreading it. It makes me sick to my stomach even thinking about."

Her dark brows draw together. "Are you sure you have to tell them? You don't want to try out my unhealthy method?"

"It's different for me. You don't struggle with asserting yourself. You're not weak and scared like I am."

She sets her hand on mine and gives it a squeeze. "I don't know where you got the idea that you're weak. You're a softie, but you have a spine of steel. I've never seen you back down when you think something is right."

Warmth washes over me. "That's maybe the sweetest thing you've ever said to me."

She squeezes my hand. "It's the absolute truth. Alright, let's get inside. I'm about to pee my pants after all that beer."

As soon as we walk inside my house, we make our way quietly up the stairs. Just as I'm about to walk into my bedroom, Vanessa's door opens. She walks out into the hallway and gives both Mari and I an up-and-down look. "Are you drunk?" she asks me.

I frown. "I drove."

She crosses her arms over her chest. "Well, you said you want to be *adventurous*, and Mari drives drunk all the time."

I glare at her. "Stop."

"Stop what?"

"You're being snotty." I take a step in her direction. "I was going to invite you to hang out with us in my room so I could give you guys all the details about my conversation with Cole, but I'm not going to if this is how you're going to act. Is that what you want? Do you want me to keep things between me and Mari from now on?"

Her frown falters, and God help me, she almost looks like she wants to cry. Why does this have to be so hard? Why do two of the three most important people in my life seem like they're going to crumble if I make a few changes? It doesn't bode well for when I tell my parents everything.

"No, I don't want that," she says, her eyes fixed on the carpet.

My frown softens. "I don't either."

She meets my gaze. "Can I still hang out with you guys? I bought some Flaming Hot Cheetos earlier. I can grab them if Mari has the drunken munchies."

"Ness, you know the key to my heart," Mari says, "and if you go get me a Dr. Pepper from the pantry, I'll forgive you for saying I drive drunk all the time."

Vanessa nods frantically before brushing past us. As soon as she makes it to the staircase, I turn to Mari and shoot her an exasperated smile. "All the time," I whisper. "You drive drunk *all the time.*"

She laughs quietly. "I've literally never driven drunk once. And how would she know? Is she spying on me?"

I shake my head and walk into my room. Goodness, my baby sister is not taking any of this well.

A couple of minutes later, we're all sitting on my bed with a bowl of bright-red Cheetos between us.

"Okay, I've waited long enough." Mari grabs a handful from the bowl. "Tell us what happened."

A smile tugs at my lips. "I had my first kiss."

"What?" Mari shouts, and I giggle and reach forward to put my hand over her mouth, which sends her into a fit of silent laughter.

"No way!" Vanessa whisper shouts.

"How was it?" Mari asks.

I sigh heavily as a visceral memory floods my senses. Cole's big, warm hands on my waist and in my hair. That delicious groan that filled my belly with heat. "Magical."

"I knew it! So does this mean he said yes?"

Her question pulls me out of my daze. "No, sadly. But he did say he would think about it. He was definitely weirded out when I asked him, but I expected that."

"I told you he wouldn't say no," Mari says. "He probably just didn't want to seem too eager by saying yes right away."

"Did he tell you how long he needs to think about it?" Vanessa asks.

"No, but I'm not going to just sit quietly and wait." I pop a Cheeto into my mouth. "He agreed to keep me safe while I do the other things on my contract." I look at Mari. "He even said he'd come out with us to the bars tomorrow night. He wants to stay sober so he can make sure I'm safe."

Mari snorts. "'Keep you safe' means he's not going to let any other guy come near you."

"No." My voice is firm. "I specifically told him he can't do that. I even told him he's gone a little overboard with his protectiveness in the past."

Mari's eyes widen. "No way! You really are asserting yourself."

I smile. "I'm trying."

"I wish I could go with you guys," Vanessa says. "Even if it's just to people-watch all the drunken college students."

She hugs her knees, drawing my gaze to her Spiderman pajama shorts. Goodness, I think those were my gift to her on her eleventh birthday. An ache tugs at my chest. In some ways, she's wiser than her seventeen years, but she's still very much my baby sister, and it must be scary for her to see her role model change.

I lift my hand and run it through her long dark hair. "I'll tell you every detail when I get home."

"I invited Travis, too." Mari's brow furrows. "I think he likes you, Livvy. I think maybe he even liked you back when he went to First Covenant."

I frown. "Why do you think that?"

"He remembered all kinds of things about you, like how much you love *Lord of the Rings*. I don't even remember hanging out with him very much at youth group. He was friends with all the bad kids."

I smile. "You became one of those bad kids."

Her grin matches mine. "After years of trying, yes, I finally did."

"Are you guys talking about Travis Anderson?" Vanessa leans forward. "I thought he was cute. I mean, not really my type, but cute."

Mari's nose wrinkles. "Not my type either. Too lanky. I like 'em big and burly like Cole and Zac."

"I think he's cute too," I say to my sister. "Maybe he can be my first drunken make-out partner. I'd probably feel more comfortable with him than a stranger at the bar."

"I think that's a great idea." Mari's smile grows. "Cole is going to hate it.'"

SIX

Cole

I'M SHAKING.

It's been hours since my conversation with Livvy, and just thinking about it makes my whole body tremble.

Ancient fantasies of her are racing through my mind. Images of those thick thighs spread open for me. Of her pretty mouth wrapped around my cock while she stares up at me with those big brown eyes. These thoughts usually only break through the darkness of my consciousness in moments of complete abandon. But they race through my head now as I stand in my kitchen while my party is winding down around me.

This isn't good.

I need to do something, or else I won't be able to resist her.

Fuck, who can I call right now? I should have thought about it earlier. It would have been easy to find a hot girl at the party, but I'd been too consumed by thoughts of her...

Someone I've already fucked won't be distracting enough. I'd probably imagine she's Livvy, which would make me feel like a piece of shit. I need novelty if I'm going to get her out of my head.

I glance into my living room where two of my friends are passed out. They won't notice if I leave now. It's only midnight. I have plenty of time to find someone at a bar, especially if I work fast.

A little while later, I'm in the backseat of an Uber and headed back home after less than an hour in a bar downtown. The beautiful brunette straddling my lap presses a kiss against my neck before inhaling softly. "You smell good."

The words send a jolt of heat into my groin. Livvy has said that to me countless times, especially when I wear cologne. She never means for it to turn me on, but it always does. She's even put her nose up to my chest and inhaled, humming afterward—

Fuck.

I'm thinking about her again.

Why did I have to find another short, curvy brunette? I should have forced myself to only approach women who look nothing like her.

Sophia presses a trail of soft kisses from my neck to my jaw. When she licks my ear, I hold back a groan. "Do that again," I whisper.

She smiles against my skin. This time I can't help but groan as her slippery tongue heats the inside of my ear. I pull her close and place a kiss on her collarbone. "Good girl," I say quietly.

"Mmm," she hums. "I'm going to be a bad girl for you soon."

A pleasant shiver runs through my body. I work my mouth down lower until I'm flush with her cleavage. God, these tits are perfect, and the belly under my hand is soft, just like Livvy's.

I'm forced to pull away from her when the Uber driver stops in front of the gate at the entrance to my parents' property. I tell him to drive up to the post so I can punch in the code. I'm just about to roll down the window when Sophia jerks in my arms. "Holy shit!"

I turn to her, frowning. "What?"

"This house. That 'W'..." She stares at the curling letter on the iron gate.

"For Walker. It's my last name."

She stares at it for several seconds with an unreadable expression. "Are you related to Mark Walker?"

A buzzing sounds in my ears, pulling me back to that moment long ago when I opened that hotel room door. "He's my dad." My voice is somehow coming from outside of myself. "Why?"

She doesn't answer, and she doesn't have to.

"I need to go home," she eventually says, her voice tight.

She tells the Uber driver we need to make another stop, or at least, I think she does. I hardly hear her.

Oh my God, he fucked her.

And not just fucked her... He fucked her somewhere in our family home. Maybe even in my parents' bed. He actually had the audacity to bring one of his women into my mom's private space.

How could he do that to her?

I should be disgusted, like I always am when I hear whispers of his affairs from people who don't know he's my dad.

What is this strange aura settling over my body and making my teeth chatter? It's faraway because I'm drunk, but I think it's panic.

This feels eerily similar to that night five years ago. I

couldn't even move after I caught him fucking that woman. I must have sensed that my life was about to change.

Nothing felt the same after my dad and I came home from that trip. It was like the world had become a shade dimmer, and only I noticed. It left me disoriented and off-kilter. Inside jokes with my friends weren't funny anymore. High school drama suddenly seemed so stupid and insignificant. I couldn't even remember why I ever cared about it before. Even baseball, which meant everything to me back then, seemed like a silly remnant from my childhood that I refused to let go, like a grungy stuffed animal.

But why am I feeling it all now? My mom is going to be fine. Pretty soon, she'll be free of him. He won't be able to hurt her with his recklessness.

Or maybe years of mistreatment has permanently damaged her.

It seems like only seconds later we're pulling up in front of an apartment complex. Thank God.

I turn to Sophia but can't find the right words. She waits for me silently.

When I'm finally able to speak, the words are clipped. "I'm sorry."

She frowns. "For what?"

My mind goes blank. "I'm not sure."

Just as she sets her hand on the door handle, I grip her forearm gently, and she turns to me. "I don't know how well you know him," I say, "but he's a piece of shit, and you deserve better."

She opens her mouth and closes it. Is she questioning how much she should tell me? "We only...hung out once. He seemed like a nice guy. You actually remind me of him now that I think about it."

That buzzing starts again. My throat is too tight to speak, so I only nod. In what feels like a flash, she's gone.

I shouldn't pity myself. In a way, I ought to be thankful for my cheating, piece-of-shit dad. If I hadn't walked in on him all those years ago, I never would have felt that strange, itching need for escape. That uncomfortable feeling that made me convince my mom to let me transfer to a public school to see if a change of scenery would make it go away.

That led me to *her*, as if we were destined to be.

Livvy was like an angel coming into my life to rescue me. She was so soft and sweet and caring, I finally had someone to talk to. I laughed again. I finally started getting excited about college and my future. Her presence alone made the world bright again.

I can't ever lose her.

Why the fuck did I tell her I'd think about her proposition? I should have told her no the second she asked me. Sex will complicate our relationship in a way I won't be able to undo. Romantic feelings would probably enter in for both of us. How could they not when we already care for each other so much?

None of it would last. Romantic feelings would fade away, and she'd go back to her old life. Marry her perfect Christian guy, and I'd become part of her past. Her former best friend and ex-lover.

No matter how tempted I am to give in, I have to do everything in my power to resist her.

SEVEN

Livvy

"LIVVY!" Mari calls from outside the dressing room. "Do you need help?"

"No, I've got it." I strip down to just my panties since I probably won't be able to wear a bra. Before grabbing the black dress Mari picked out for me, I stare at my body in the mirror for a moment.

Why do my boobs have to be so big and unsightly? They hang down almost to my belly. You'd think I had three kids.

Cole is standing right outside. Every flaw will be on display for his eyes.

I grit my teeth as I slip the tight fabric up my thighs, over my belly, and up to my chest. Goodness, I hate how the fabric clings to my every curve.

After pulling on the last strap, I keep my gaze away from the mirror. If I look at myself, I might chicken out. I already want to cringe at how the air hits my chest with this plunge neckline. It makes me feel disgusting.

In theory, I know I don't really look disgusting, but this is the problem with sexual shame. It's visceral. How can you talk yourself out of something you feel in your body? It's like trying to reason away a fever.

"Is it on?" Mari shouts.

"Yes...unfortunately."

"I don't want to hear any of that. That's our old youth pastor talking, making you feel ashamed for simply having breasts."

A smile rises to my lips. "This is more than having breasts. This dress is practically lingerie."

"Yes," Mari shouts. "That's exactly why I picked it. Okay, give us a runway walk."

"I'll give you guys a quick look, and that's it. Mari, you can come in here if you want to get a better view of it."

"Come on, Liv. You know Cole has been dying to see your beautiful boobs since the moment he met you."

Cole chuckles, but I get the sense that he's uncomfortable, and a smile rises to my lips. Goodness, Mari is so bold. She's the ideal person to help me through this whole process. I need her to push me.

"My boobs are a problem in this dress." I try to keep my voice low while still projecting it out of the dressing room. "I can't wear a bra, and, Mari, you know how they don't stay in one place without one. They keep moving around, and I'm worried someone's going to see my..." I lower my voice to just above a whisper, "nipples."

Mari cackles. "You have to see Cole's face right now. It's bright red."

"Aww, I'm sorry, Cole."

His laughter sounds a little forced. "It's okay. I can go outside and wait if you want."

"No, don't do that. I highly doubt I'm going to buy this one, but I still want your opinion on it."

I have to do this. If I can't even show my body off in a dress, how can I ever expect to get naked in front of him? I straighten my spine and open the curtain.

Cole and Mari stand only a few feet away, and both of their heads perk up. I make my way out of the dressing room toward Mari. I can't look at Cole's face. Not yet.

"Oh my God!" Mari's lips part into an open-mouthed grin. "This is it. This is the dress. You look like a goddess. I'm not kidding."

When I start to complain, she halts me with her hand. "Don't! Just listen to me first."

I close my mouth and exhale heavily through my nose.

She looks at me probingly. "Your boobs look amazing. You understand that, right? Even if you don't feel like it?"

"Sort of."

"No, not sort of. You know. In your heart of hearts, you know your boobs look amazing. Just imagine if they were someone else's boobs. Would you think they looked good?"

"I don't know..."

"Think of Brenna. She has boobs like yours. Do you think they look good on her?"

My brow knits as Mariana's short and curvy friend flashes in my mind. I guess she does have a similar body type, and she often wears shirts that show her cleavage. "Yeah, she does have really nice boobs."

"See! You do understand." She places her soft hands on my cheeks and forces me to look up at her. "You not wanting to show off your boobs is not you. It's a youth pastor telling you your T-shirts are too tight and causing the boys to stumble in their faith. Your body remembers being told those things, even if you don't agree with them now."

She's right. She's absolutely right.

"Cole, can I get your help?" Mari places both hands on my shoulders and twists me around. "Tell her how good her boobs look."

It takes me a moment before I can look up at his face, but when I do, a pleasant tingle runs over my skin. His lips are slightly parted, and his wide eyes are fixed on my chest. He's never looked at me like that before.

Strangely, I don't want to cover my chest like I thought I would. The look in his eyes makes me feel almost...

Powerful.

"Cole," Mari's voice is almost a shout this time, and he snaps his gaze up to her face.

"Yeah..." He lifts his hand and scratches the back of his head. "She looks beautiful. She always looks beautiful."

"No." Mari shakes her head sharply. "Don't minimize it. You know this dress is on a whole other level, and I asked you specifically about her boobs. She's self-conscious about them. We were raised to think that our bodies are sinful. Livvy especially got hit hard with it, because she developed when we were really young. Tell her how luscious and gorgeous they are. How you want to squeeze them."

I snort out a laugh. "Mari, stop."

She looks at me sternly. "When you wear this out tonight, people are going to be staring at your boobs. They won't be able to help it. How are you going to handle it if you're too embarrassed to let Cole look at them?"

"I just don't want him to feel forced to say—"

"I don't feel forced, Livvy." When I glance at Cole, his eyes are almost dazed. They drop to my chest, and that achy heat fills my belly once again. "You look...gorgeous. Fucking goddamn..." He shakes his head.

I can't stop the grin from spreading across my face, even though it probably makes me look girlish. "Well, in that case, I'll get the dress." I turn to Mari, frowning. "But what am I going to do about my boobs? They move around too much. How can I stop them from falling out?"

"I've got you covered. We'll tape them."

I wince. "It always looks so painful when you tape yours."

"It's not at all. Trust me. And you'll feel supported. We'll push them up like this—" she cups my boobs and smashes them together, "—to give you the best cleavage. What do you think, Cole?"

A little laugh is pulled from my chest, and when I glance at Cole, his eyes are molten again.

"She looks great." His voice is breathy.

My goodness, he really likes how I look in this dress. Maybe I wasn't reading too much into that kiss.

Maybe he really does want me.

"Okay," I say. "But where are we going to get ready? I really don't want my parents seeing me dressed like this. Not yet. Honestly, I'm not even comfortable with your parents seeing me. Or your abuela. It's silly, but I know how disappointed they'll be in me, and I love them so much. It'll make me sad and just throw off my whole vibe for tonight, you know?"

Mari nods slowly. "And you know my dad will tell your dad."

I smile sadly. "They're going to start praying for both of us."

"Why don't you guys get ready at my place?" Cole says. "I can stay out of your way when you... You know... Tape her up. I'll make you guys dinner." He looks at Mari, his brows drawing together. "We need to make sure she eats a full meal before we go out. I don't want her getting drunk too fast."

Mari nods. "Lots of protein. She's going to want carbs—"

"You guys," I interrupt, rolling my eyes.

Their heads snap in my direction, as if they'd forgotten I was here.

"I appreciate how much you're both looking out for me, but I don't think either of you had anyone acting like this the first time you got drunk, and you both turned out just fine. I want to feel like a regular college student. Let me have a wild night. If I get drunk too fast because I didn't eat enough protein, that's on me. Let me suffer the consequences of my actions, like you two have on nights when you've had too much to drink."

Mari opens her mouth to speak, but Cole talks over her. "We agreed I'll look out for you so that you can relax and have a good time, and that's what I'm going to do. I'm not letting you get sick."

I sigh, not wanting to get into an argument with him when it's a reasonable expectation. Still, it would be nice if he framed it as a request instead of a command. I smile warmly at him. "That's very thoughtful."

His expression softens. "I just want you to have fun."

"I know you do." When I reach out and touch his arm, his body goes rigid at first, but then it relaxes, and his gaze drifts to my chest.

Wow. This is new. I don't think I've ever caught him staring at my boobs before, let alone three times in five minutes.

"If you really want Livvy to have a good time, you should invite some of your hot friends. Ooh, maybe we could even pre-party at your place?"

Cole's posture grows rigid. "I don't want to make her nervous with too many people."

I shake my head. "It won't. I want to force myself to socialize more." I look at Mari. "We could have Travis meet us there instead of at the bars."

Cole's jaw ticks. "Travis is coming out tonight?"

Mari nods. "Livvy's considering him for her first drunken make-out session, but we also talked about Zac."

Cole's eyebrows shoot to the top of his forehead. "She is *not* making out with Zac."

"Why not?" Mari asks.

His expression grows incredulous. "He's one of my best friends."

"What difference does that make?" Her tone is suspiciously earnest.

When Cole's eyes widen and then grow dazed, I take it as my cue to step in.

"I won't make out with Zac. I can see how that would make you uncomfortable."

His expression softens. "No, it's okay. I trust Zac. And if you're going to..." He inhales a deep breath before giving me a hard stare. "If you're going to do this, I'd rather it be with people I trust. I can even invite over a few of my old baseball buddies. I would trust any of them with my life."

Mari smiles wide. "Livvy, if you could pick from the base-ball team like they were a box of truffles, which ones would you select?"

"Hmm... Theo's really cute."

Cole's mouth tightens. "You called Theo a man-whore."

I scowl. "The old judgmental Livvy said things like that. Now I would say that he has sex like a normal person." I shoot Mari a saucy smile. "Guys who have lots of sex are probably good at kissing, right?"

She smiles back. "Absolutely. If you know how to move your dick, you know how to move your tongue. The two things go hand in hand."

When I giggle, Cole steps forward, his expression tight.

"Mari, let's not push her with all this stuff. We need her to take it slow."

A hint of a smile touches Mari's lips. "*We* need that? Why do we need that?"

His nostrils flare. "She's shy. We don't want her—"

"*We*," Mari interrupts. "You keep saying that like we're on the same page, and we're not. *I* want her to break out of her shell. *You* seem like you don't want her to. In fact, whenever she's around other guys, you look like you want to lock her up."

He huffs out a laugh, but the sound of it is brittle.

"It's okay. I know you're just worried about me," I say to Cole, though I'm starting to wonder if maybe it's more complicated than that. "Tonight, I'll just focus on getting drunk and flirting. I'll only make out with someone if it feels right."

His jaw clenches. "And I'll be right there if you need me. I'll make sure you're safe."

I smile. "Thank you, Daddy."

He averts his gaze from mine and exhales an unsteady breath.

Cole

HER SOFT VOICE floats into my kitchen, and my whole body relaxes. I can't quite make out what she's saying over the sizzling bacon, but I can tell just from her tone that she's really trying to assert herself. She's spoken much more than she normally does when she's in a group of guys. Whenever I've brought her around my male friends before, she's stayed glued to my side as if she might get devoured by a wild animal if I left her alone. Fuck, she's so sweet.

And so vulnerable.

There are three guys in there, all of whom I know well, and I still can't relax.

Why do I want to hit something?

It's good that she's putting herself out there and pushing through her shyness. I'm a selfish bastard for wanting her to be the way she was before—sitting so close our legs were almost touching and reserving her smiles only for me when I turned and talked softly to her.

If I could only say yes to her proposition, none of this would be happening. There would be no point in inviting guys over. I could give her everything.

God fucking damn it, why does she have to be so tempting? I can't have her that way. It will put me on the path toward losing her forever.

When the bacon strips are nearly black at the edges, I scoop them up and plop them onto a plate. I march out into my small living room. All three guys are standing around where she sits on the couch. Her tits are practically falling out of that dress, even with all the tape Mari put on them, but I can't let myself look at them again.

I might lose my mind.

I set the plate down on the coffee table in front of her. "I want you to eat all of this before we leave."

Her brow knits. "You were making that bacon for me?"

I shrug. "You love it."

"I mean... Yeah, but I already had dinner."

"You picked at it. You barely ate anything, and we ate way too early. You need something more before you start drinking."

She frowns. "I don't think I can eat all of it. Do you mind if I share it with everyone?"

"Don't argue with Daddy," Mari says.

Livvy smiles up at me. "Are you going to spank me if I don't eat every bite?"

When chuckles break out, Livvy's grin widens, and my heart squeezes in my chest. Oh God, I don't even think she realizes how sexual that sounded. She just thinks it's funny because her insane parents actually spanked her until she was thirteen years old. She has no clue that every guy in this room is probably imagining doing it to her now. I can't stand this. I want to haul her away from here.

With effort, I shoot her a reassuring smile. "Eat as much as you can." *Be a good girl for me.* The words hover on the tip of my tongue, as they always do when she unintentionally turns me on.

"Alright!" Mari claps her hands. "Daddy Cole, you need to give her some room if we're going to get her out of her shell tonight. Livvy's goal is to have a wild, hot-girl summer. She's finally living like a regular college student, and we're going to help her. We're going to get her to flirt tonight. She doesn't know how, and it's not her fault. It's a Christian thing. We were taught to evangelize, which is the opposite of flirting."

"Yep," Travis says. "It's why we're all socially awkward."

Mari nods. "You can all help her practice by flirting like crazy with her."

Theo looks at me, his eyes wide. "Are you okay with this?"

Heat washes over my skin. I'm about to answer when Zac bursts into laughter. "No fucking way, dude." He's still chuckling as he looks at Livvy. "Don't get me wrong, I would love to flirt with you, but I'm going to self-eliminate. Cole would kill me. *Literally* kill me."

"No, I wouldn't." I glare at him. "I've only been protective of her in the past because she didn't want the attention. Now she does, and I'd rather you flirt with her than a stranger at the bar."

Zac snorts. "A stranger at the bar. God have mercy on his

soul. You are very hot, Livvy, but I'm not risking my life just to flirt with you. Now, Mariana on the other hand..."

"No." Mari shakes her head. "Tonight's about Livvy. I'm going to busy finding guys for her."

"I'm happy to volunteer," Travis says, and my jaw clenches.

"Thank you, Travis," Mari says. "Why don't you start by sitting next to Livvy?"

"Jesus, Mari," I can't help but burst out. "Can't you just let it happen naturally? This is awkward as fuck for everyone."

She glares at me, but something that looks like mischief sparks in her eyes.

Goddamn her, she's doing this just to annoy me. Mari's always known how to get under my skin when it comes to Livvy. She probably senses that I'm hanging on by a thread, that it's killing me not to order the guys to stay away from her.

Livvy turns to me, laughter dancing in her eyes. "It's okay. I'm having fun."

The tension leaves my shoulders at the delight in her voice. I can do this. I can get through the night, especially if she's having fun. What are the odds that she's actually going to make out with someone? Slim to none. She can't change who she is in one night.

Livvy glances at Travis and then Theo. "You can both sit next to me."

The guys grin, like they're charmed by her awkward little suggestion. How could they not be? She doesn't have to be good at flirting when she's the most adorable person in the world.

Both of the guys plop down on the couch, scooting close to her afterward, and something churns in my stomach. Fuck, I don't like this.

Livvy smiles up at Zac. "I would invite you too, but you already said no to flirting, and there's no more room."

Zac grins at her. "That's okay, sweetheart. I like my life."

I roll my eyes. "Zac, that joke is getting old."

"It's not a joke," Mari says, shooting me a hard look. "I want to talk to both of you for a second." Before I get a chance to speak, Mari grabs Zac and I and drags us into the kitchen. I can't stop my gaze from drifting back into the living room.

Travis is leaning in close to Livvy, and she's smiling up at him.

"She's fine."

My gaze snaps to Mari's face. "What do you want to talk about?"

"This." She gestures at me. "You're hovering over Livvy, and it needs to stop."

"I was literally just standing there."

She rolls her eyes. "No, you weren't. Zac, was he hovering?"

"Yes," he answers immediately. "He always hovers over her."

I scowl at him. "What the fuck does that even mean?"

"You give her no space," Mari says. "You stand right next to her. You insert yourself into all her conversations."

"So I'm acting like normal fucking human beings do when they hang out with people?"

"You don't look like a normal human being." She gestures at me. "You're huge. What guy is going to be brave enough to approach her at the bar when her glaring six-foot-five body-guard is hovering?"

I raise both hands into the air. "What exactly am I supposed to do about that? I can't help that I'm tall."

Mari's expression grows exasperated and she glances at Zac. "Please help me."

"Do what we're doing right now," he says. "Stay back a little bit. Maybe find your own girl tonight—"

"Absolutely not," I say. "I'm not leaving her alone her first time out drinking."

Mari's eyelids flutter dramatically. "Okay, I think we're talking in circles here."

Livvy's giggle floats into the kitchen, and my chest grows heavy. That was genuine laughter. Livvy will laugh at anything. She's always so worried about hurting people's feelings, and when they tell dumb jokes, she gives a forced giggle.

That wasn't it though.

I only hear that laugh when it's just the two of us.

When I glance into the living room, she's smiling shyly at Travis. "I don't know if you have a good heart, but I don't have any reason to think you don't."

Mari sucks in her lips to fight a smile, her expression growing almost pained. "A good heart?" she whispers. "Did she really just say that? Oh my God, my bestie is precious."

Heat pulses through my veins as I strain to listen over Mari's voice.

"I wish I had talked to you more," Travis says. "I bet I seemed like a dirtbag back then."

"No, not at all." Livvy's tone is urgent. "I was really judgmental of the kids I thought were rebellious, but that was mostly because they intimidated me."

"Did I intimidate you?" Travis leans in so close his forehead is practically touching hers.

"A little bit." She averts her gaze from his, clearly uncomfortable with his closeness.

When I take a step toward the living room, Mari grabs my forearm. "Don't you dare."

I lift a hand in the air. "I was literally just going to walk in there. It's weird that we're all whispering over here."

"Stay." She delivers the word through clenched teeth.

I exhale a shaky breath. Fuck, this is so hard. Why am I so territorial with her?

"I promise you I'm just another awkward Christian," Travis says, and the gentleness in his tone makes me want to roll my eyes. He's putting on a show for Livvy. I've never heard him talk about being religious before.

"If I seemed rebellious," Travis says, "it's because I'm a huge try-hard."

Livvy giggles again. She loves it when people make fun of themselves. It endears them to her.

Goddamn Travis.

Theo walks into the kitchen and I spear him with a hard look. "What are you doing?" I ask.

"It seems like they're hitting it off," he says. "I thought I'd give them some alone time." He frowns. "Isn't that what you guys are doing?"

"We're trying," Mari says, glaring at me. "Not everyone wants to give her alone time."

Theo snorts. "I can't believe you're allowing this. I always thought she was...your girlfriend, basically. Or that she'd be your girlfriend as soon as you're ready to get married."

I avert my gaze. "I'm never getting married. I don't even believe in monogamy."

"Okay, Cole," Mari says. "We don't need to hear your whole fuck-boy manifesto." She looks at Theo and then Zac. "Livvy's not planning on waiting until marriage anymore. She wants to lose her virginity this summer."

"*Jesus*," I whisper shout. "We don't need to tell the whole world."

Mari waves a hand at me, not even glancing my way. "Livvy's not keeping it a secret. She actually wants to make out with someone tonight. If Travis doesn't make a move, maybe one of you could—"

"We're not doing that," I say. "We agreed not to push her."

Mari glares at me. "She's already had her first kiss."

"With me." My voice feels like it's coming from outside of my body. "She had her first kiss with me, because she trusts me."

The kitchen grows quiet. Good God, what came over me?

"Holy shit," Zac says. "When did this happen?"

I look away, unable to meet his eyes. Fuck, he's never going to let this go. Now that he knows I kissed her, he's going to harass me endlessly.

When I'm finally able to look at Mari, her grin makes heat break out over my skin. She knows what that was. She knows I was making sure they all know who she really belongs to.

She doesn't, though. Why can't I stop these impulses when I know they're irrational?

"Livvy," Mari calls out to the living room. "Hurry up and scarf your bacon so we can head to the bar." She looks at Travis. "Do you want to be her gentleman escort?"

"I'm driving her," I say.

"No, Daddy Cole." Mari says. "It's time to let the little one leave the nest."

I roll my eyes. "Mari, the whole Daddy Cole thing is really starting to creep me out."

"Only when I say it." Her eyelids grow lazy "You love it when she calls you Daddy."

When the guys chuckle quietly, I look away. Holy fuck, how am I going to get through the night?

EIGHT

Livvy

AS SOON AS we park on State Street, Travis turns to me. "So what's up with you and Cole?"

I force a smile as my gut sinks. I hate having to explain why Cole's overprotectiveness doesn't mean he wants me.

"Nothing," I say. "We're just very close, and he's always been protective of me."

Travis's eyes widen. "He's, like, insane. What was with the bacon and him telling you that you have to eat it all? Is he your nutritionist?"

My smile grows. "I know. Honestly though, he's like that with everyone."

"No." Travis shakes his head. "I mean, I haven't hung out with him a ton since he left for college, but every time I have, he's had a girl with him, and he was never like that with any of them."

"Well, you probably haven't seen him with his brother or

sister. He can be really bossy with them too, but he doesn't mean to be. He has a really kind and caring heart."

Travis smiles. "You're sweet. So does that mean you're kind of like a sister to him?"

I open my mouth and close it as something flutters in my belly. A few days ago, I wouldn't have hesitated to say yes, and just saying that small word would've left me dejected, but now I'm not so sure. Maybe I'm inexperienced, but he really seemed to like kissing me, and he wasn't able to keep his eyes off my chest today.

Maybe he's starting to see me as a sexual being rather than a naive little girl.

"We have a really close platonic friendship," I say, because it's the truth.

Even though I hope it might change one day.

Travis grins. "Can I kiss you then?"

Heat washes over my face. My gaze is drawn to the passenger window and the people walking by on the sidewalk.

I can do this.

I lick my bottom lip, my heart starting to race. I put my palm over my mouth. "I just ate ten pieces of bacon."

Travis stares at me blankly for a moment before a smile spreads over his face. "I don't mind. I love bacon."

A tight smile twitches at my lips, and I curse myself for my nervousness. I'm twenty-one years old, for crying out loud. I should be long accustomed to kisses in the car.

I have to do this. This is the part of being young that I've been missing out on all these years.

"Do you have a mint?" My voice is small.

As if snapping out of a daze, Travis's eyes pop open and start darting around his car. He opens his glove compartment and rustles around a bit before going to the center console and throwing objects into the backseat by the handful. "Fuck," he finally says. "I'll be right back."

He hops out of the car and darts down the sidewalk in the direction of the corner gas station. Goodness, he really wants to kiss me. I ought to be flattered, and yet sickness stirs in my stomach.

It seems like less than a minute has passed before Travis jogs back to the car. He's a little out of breath as he hops in and tosses a small green square on my lap.

"Trident." I unwrap the gum and pop a square into my mouth. "It reminds me of my grandma."

A small smile tugs at Travis's lips. "That's exactly what I wanted to do—remind you of your grandma right before I kiss you."

A hysterical giggle is pulled from my chest, nervousness prickling like wildfire over my skin now that the moment has come.

"I'm sorry if I'm overly eager," he says.

I shake my head jerkily. "You're fine. It's just that I'm a twenty-one-year-old virgin, and even something as small as a kiss makes me really nervous."

"Yeah..." His eyes look almost dazed. "I can't believe you're still a virgin. I thought everyone at First Covenant was full of shit about all that waiting-until-marriage stuff. I definitely was. One time, I even fingered my girlfriend in the parking lot after youth group."

My eyes must be huge, because he grins and squeezes my hand. "I hope you don't think less of me."

"I don't. It's healthy to explore your sexuality when you're young. But hearing things like that always makes me feel...so behind. I'm such an outlier, even compared to other Christians my age. You've all lived these full lives that I can't relate to."

"There's plenty of time to catch up."

When I glance up, he's leaning forward. His eyes are molten, and it brings me back to that moment just before Cole kissed me. There's a churning in my gut when our lips touch, but it's okay. How can I enjoy a kiss when I'm this nervous? Travis nibbles on my lip before slipping his tongue inside my mouth. On impulse, I pull back.

"Too much?" he asks.

"No." I swallow. "It was fine."

When I shoot him my best smile, his face falls. "Oh God, that was a bad kiss, huh? That's what you're thinking. I can tell that's what you're thinking."

His vulnerability washes away all my nervousness. This I can handle. I set my hand on his. "No, it's not that. Honestly, I'm so nervous that I'm in my head."

"That's not a good sign. A good kiss should take you out of your head. It probably means you don't have chemistry with me."

Goodness, I used to employ this same kind of romantic thinking with Cole. He couldn't care for me so much, couldn't be so protective and make me such a priority in his life if he didn't have some kind of deep feelings for me. He couldn't be everything I wanted in a husband—strong and commanding but also sweet and thoughtful—if God hadn't designed him for me.

"I reject that kind of thinking," I say, "and you should too."

His brow knits. "What do you mean?"

"Not everything is black and white. All or nothing. I only had my first kiss recently because I thought even one sexual encounter would taint my purity."

Travis cringes. "Yeah, I find all that stuff creepy now."

"It's really creepy, and so is thinking one awkward kiss means two people don't have chemistry."

He chuckles. "I'm not sure if that makes me feel better, but I'll take it."

I smile warmly. I didn't expect him to be so vulnerable.

"Can we go inside now?" I ask. "I'm thinking maybe I'll be less nervous after a drink."

He squeezes my hand. "Sure. Let's get you good and drunk."

Though my stomach grows queasy at the thought, it doesn't mean I'm not going to do just that. I'll never get over this nervousness if I don't try new things.

When I step out of the car, the damp ocean air hits my chest, sending a wave of tingling shame over my skin. When I look down at my boobs, a strip of nude tape is visible on my right side. I take a moment to adjust myself before looking up.

My stomach drops.

Cole is standing with his back against the concrete wall of the bar. His jaw is set, and his eyes are blazing. I don't even need to ask if he saw Travis and I kiss in the car.

Cole

A RAGING heat pulses through my veins. Oh fuck, I can't do this. I can't stand by and watch her kiss other guys.

I'm going to lose my mind.

Those big brown eyes widen as she strides in my direction. Travis walks closely beside her. Too close, like he thinks he owns her.

She's mine.

Why can't I keep these territorial impulses in check? For years, I've prepared myself for the day she'd meet her perfect Christian guy. I knew I'd have to plant a smile on my face and force myself to get to know him, even as I wanted to punch his asshole face.

I would get over it eventually. There's no way I could let possessiveness jeopardize the most perfect thing in my life, especially if she found someone who made her really happy.

At least, that's what I told myself.

Oh God, what if I can't? Watching someone else press his lips against hers was agony, and Travis isn't even a real threat. He says he's religious, but he's nothing like her. She would never consider him for anything long term.

I have to get this under control. With effort, I smile as she approaches me. "I already know what I'm ordering for your first drink."

She smiles back. "That sounds—"

"No, I called it already."

I turn toward Travis. "You called what?"

"Her first drink." His words are matter of fact. "I called it in the car."

I frown. "Are you seven years old?"

A small smile tugs at his lips. "I'm getting her a Mai Tai. She loves fruity drinks."

I shake my head sharply. "A Mai Tai is way too strong for her."

"I—" Livvy starts but then closes her mouth when Travis starts talking.

"Dude, you already force-fed her bacon. I think she's fine now, Daddy Cole."

Daddy Cole. He's just trying to goad me, probably because he knows I saw that kiss. Travis always pulls shit like this. He gets under people's skin for fun. Why didn't I notice what a dick he is before tonight?

I take a deep breath and turn to Livvy. "I'll get you a strawberry daiquiri later, okay?" I look at her sternly. "In an hour. You're only having one drink an hour."

When she sucks in her lips to fight a smile, heat creeps into my cheeks. "I just don't want you to get sick."

She smiles in earnest now, and her chest shakes with silent laughter. "I know."

I exhale. "I'm sorry. I'm not used to having you out at the bars with me, but I promise I'll stay back and let you have a good time."

Travis pats my shoulder. "Why don't you start now? I'll take her in. How about you drive my car to my apartment? It's literally two minutes from here, and my roommate can drive you back."

I stare at him blankly. When he lifts his keys in my direction, heat washes over my skin. "Are you fucking kidding me?"

"No." He shrugs. "I don't want it to get stolen, and you're staying sober, so what else are you going to do?"

"I'm not your fucking valet. You can drive it yourself."

A faint smile twinges his lips. "Nah, I'm ready to drink, and she's having a good time with me. Don't kill the vibe."

When he sets his hand on her shoulder, I clench my teeth to fight the childish urge to reach out and pull her away from him.

Why am I letting him do this? He's almost laughing he's enjoying my irritation so much.

"'Don't kill the vibe'?" I frown. "You sound like a fucking idiot—"

"Cole, enough!"

Livvy's uncharacteristic shout startles me, and when I glance at her, my stomach sinks. Oh God, I hate it when she looks at me like that. It's so rare that it happens, and it means I really fucked up.

Her frown deepens. "I'm getting sick to death of hearing

you both argue like little boys. You weren't even letting me talk."

Travis chuckles. "I'm sorry, Livvy. I was just fucking with h—"

"Let me finish! I need a minute away from both of you, but especially you, Cole. You keep saying over and over again that you want me to have a good time, but I don't think I believe you anymore." She crosses her arms over her chest. "It seems like you're only thinking about yourself and how *you* want things to go tonight."

"I'm sorry." My voice is soft. "I really do want you to have fun."

She stares at me for a long moment. "I think you should drive Travis's car to his place, if only to give me a few minutes to myself."

My stomach hollows. Oh God, I hate it when she banishes me from her presence. She's only done it a handful of times when she's been really angry with me, and usually never for more than a few minutes, but it always fills me with the irrational desire to throw myself at her feet and beg her to never leave me.

"I can do that."

She nods once. "I'm heading inside to find the others." When she starts toward the bar and Travis follows her, she turns to him and lifts a hand. "I want you to give me a minute, too. As someone who's been a designated driver more times than I can count, I can tell you I've felt really used when people have treated me like their chauffeur."

Travis nods quickly. "I should have thought of that."

As soon as she walks inside the bar, Travis bursts into laughter. "Dude, what just happened? Are we in time-out?" He shakes his head. "God, she's cute."

I roll my eyes, unable to even slightly share his glee when

I'm in the doghouse. "Shut up. I'm so fucking annoyed with you."

His laughter grows louder. "Thank you for calling me an idiot." He can barely get the words out as he lifts his keys in my direction. "That worked out really well for me."

I roll my eyes as I take them from his hand. "I think I might crash your car for fun."

"You do that. I'm sure your rich-ass parents have great insurance. Well, I'd better go find my girl."

He grins like a moron before turning around and walking inside the bar, and I wish I didn't want to throw his keys into the gutter. He probably only taunted me so he could tell our old baseball team that I lost my shit over a strawberry daiquiri. He isn't a real threat when it comes to Livvy, but, oh God, this is all so much harder than I thought it would be.

She's so much bolder than I expected, and now that I've been banished and forced to play valet to the douchebag who just gave her her second ever kiss, it's time to finally admit that I never thought she would really go through with any of this. I thought maybe she would have a drink or two. Maybe she would wear a dress that at least *she* considered slutty. And maybe she would flirt in her own shy way, but the rest of it... No way.

Does this mean she's really going to lose her virginity at the end of the summer to some guy she hardly knows?

It could be me.

Fuck, I need to think.

As Travis predicted, it takes me only two minutes to drive to his apartment complex. I don't bother calling his roommate after I park his car, much preferring a walk through the chilly evening air as I sort out my thoughts.

What am I going to do? I don't think I can stomach letting

her lose her virginity to a stranger, but what if I have sex with her and everything changes between us?

Both options are miserable, but I think I can predict what I'm going to do. Some deep, primitive part of me knows I won't be able to let her do it with someone else, no matter how many times I tell myself that sex could put our friendship at risk. If I have to witness any more of this—other guys touching and kissing her—I'm inevitably going to give in.

Why do I have to be like this? I've brought women around her countless times, and she's never been territorial with me. Why can't I be as mature as she is?

My head isn't any less muddled by the time I make it inside the bar. It takes me less than a minute to find her. My gaze always seems to be drawn to her like a magnet. I stand for a moment to watch her. She looks up at Travis while he talks, and her stiff posture is a sign she's nervous. This place is a lot more crowded than I expected it would be on a Thursday night. I should have picked a dive bar, if only to give her more space.

She takes a small sip of her yellow drink, and I can tell by the slight tightening of her mouth afterward that she doesn't like it. I roll my eyes. Fucking Travis. I told him the Mai Tai would be too strong for her, and she would never in a million years tell him she doesn't like it.

When I get close, she turns to me, and I shoot her a contrite smile. I raise my voice over the crowd noise. "Was that enough time, or are you still mad at me?"

She sets her soft hand on my arm, and it makes my gut clench. Her signature arm grab used to be the only kind of touch I could handle from her.

Not anymore.

"I'm not mad." She lifts her head in the direction of my ear, and even though I know she's going to tell me something, my whole body grows tense in anticipation. I've always had to brace myself whenever her mouth gets anywhere near my body.

"That was really sweet of you to take his car home." Her warm breath tickles my ear, sending tingles down my spine. "Even though he was rude."

"I deserved it." I glance at Travis and back at her. "Would you mind if we went outside and talked for a bit?"

She smiles wide, and, oh God, it's heaven to be back in her good graces. After saying something to Travis, she slips off her bar stool and starts making her way through the crowd. I set my hand on her shoulder to guide her to the back patio, and just that small touch sends electricity into my gut. After her proposition yesterday, every brush of her skin sets me on fire.

As soon as I find a secluded spot on the patio, I turn to her. "I've been really overbearing tonight, and I'm sorry. I need to give you more space."

She smiles sadly. "I only needed a minute. Of course I want to spend time with you on my first wild night out."

"Yeah, but I'm not letting you be wild. I don't know why I'm like this with you. I know being sheltered doesn't mean you need a babysitter, but I just..." I run a hand through my hair. "I don't know. I have no chill, and I hate it. I don't know what's wrong with me."

Her smile grows. "You're a very protective daddy."

I snort, shutting my eyes. Of course she would say that right now.

"I bet you like it when girls call you Daddy in the bedroom, huh?"

My eyes pop open. "What?" I nearly shout.

Her expression grows hesitant. "I was just teasing."

"Did you know that's a thing?"

Her gaze falls to the concrete. "Well, yeah. Mari's told me some things..."

"Is that what you've meant this whole time whenever you've called me Daddy?"

Her cheeks grow pink. Fuck, I'm embarrassing her, but I need to find out. I'll go crazy if I don't.

"Well, yeah," she says, "but I was just trying to be funny."

I take a deep breath to calm myself. "It is funny." *No, it's not.* "I just had no clue you were making a sexual joke."

Her brow furrows. "Sometimes it's like you think I'm a little kid. I have a lot of gaps in my knowledge because of the way I was raised, but I'm not stupid."

"Of course you're not stupid, and I *definitely* don't think you're a little kid." My gaze drifts to her chest as I reach out and touch her shoulder. "I'm sorry if I embarrassed you. I was just surprised. And for the record, I don't like being called Daddy —" I smile faintly, "—by anyone except you."

Her gaze snaps to my face, and her eyes grow wide. "Are you being serious?"

I laugh softly. "I am."

"Why only by me?"

"I don't know. It makes me feel...some things."

She takes a step in my direction. "What kind of things?"

Fuck, this is dangerous. I need to be certain this is the right thing before I start telling her what I've really been thinking all these years. "I don't want to keep you out here too long. Mari will kill me if she knows I've stolen you away from everyone."

Her face falls. She stares at me for a moment before nodding. "And I don't want Travis to think I'm ditching him. I've actually had a lot of fun with him tonight."

My spine goes rigid. "Livvy, he's a fucking idiot."

She raises her brows. "Yeah, you said that already. My

sister used to call me an idiot when she was mad. When she was in elementary school."

I smile sheepishly. "I know I acted like a child earlier, but... You're way too good for him. I've never liked him all that much. I mean, he's fine. I tolerate him, but he's not for you."

"That's for me to decide."

I grit my teeth. "He was trying to piss me off earlier. He always does that kind of shit, especially when we go out drinking. You can't stand people like that. Why would you have any interest in him?"

"He's non-threatening." Her voice is notably softer. "I'm nervous about all this. I'm nervous to get drunk. I'm nervous to kiss. It helps to hang out with someone I don't have a crazy crush on, because it lowers the pressure. I don't feel like I have to be a really good kisser."

I look away from her, not wanting her to see how much I hate this. How much the idea of her kissing another guy makes me want to throw her over my shoulder and take her away from here. "I just wish..."

"What?"

"I wish you would take my advice."

"What advice?"

"If you're really going to push through with this whole contract thing, wait until you find a guy you could actually be with long term. Maybe not for the kissing, but for losing your virginity. I know you well, and I think you'll be happier if you lose your virginity to someone you can at least see yourself being in a relationship with."

"I'm not ruling that out."

I frown. "What do you mean?"

"Maybe I could be in a relationship with Travis. It doesn't feel like it now, but I'm open to it. He and I had a nice heart-to-heart in the car."

"Livvy, he's not religious. Not like you. He hasn't mentioned God or church once in the years that I've known him."

"I know he's not, but my faith has evolved. I don't need to be with a Christian anymore."

An otherworldly energy settles over me, and my ears start to ring. "What?" My voice is a croak.

She nods like it's nothing, like she's just telling me about a movie she saw yesterday. "My partner's faith, or lack thereof, has nothing to do with mine. My relationship with Jesus is deeply personal."

"When..." I take a deep breath through my nose. "When did you decide this?"

She purses her lips to the side and narrows her eyes. "I guess it's come on slowly over this last year. I've been reflecting a lot about purity culture, and this is tied to it. I was taught that I needed a Christian husband to be my spiritual leader, and I find all of that toxic now. I need to be my own spiritual leader, so it might actually be better for me to be with someone outside of my faith, someone who can help me see other perspectives and challenge me."

I nod slowly, unable to craft a response to that. Why does it feel like the whole world shifted, just like it did years ago? Except this time, everything is glowing. Warmth rushes through my veins, and her beautiful face is sparkling. What is this feeling?

I think it might be hope.

"You really changed your mind?"

A small notch forms between her brows. "Cole..."

I swallow. "What?"

"You seem like you're really affected by what I just told you."

"Yeah," I scoff. "It's pretty big news."

She stares at me for a moment. "It's big for me, but is there a reason it's significant for you?"

Another blanket of warmth drifts over me. Oh God, I could actually be with her, just like I wanted all those years ago. But this time, I wouldn't have to go to church. I wouldn't have to resign myself to lying to her every single day by pretending like I believe in something that still feels imaginary, even after the year I spent trying to make it real. I could just...be with her.

Why am I even considering it?

I've always known that her rigid religious background is a blessing in disguise. It's the only reason I still have her in my life, so why do I feel like she opened door of possibilities?

Fuck, I need to think.

"It's a little noisy out here," I say, "and I want to give you my full attention when we talk about this. Why don't you get back in there and find the others? I'll be right in."

Something flashes across her face. It looks a little like hurt, but I can't think about that right now. I absolutely need some space to think, or I might do something really impulsive like tell her I've been waiting for this moment since the day I met her.

In a flash, she's gone. How did she leave so quickly? Fuck, the whole world is buzzing, like I've taken a strong hit from a bong.

I walk to the edge of the patio, grip the cold metal bars, and squeeze tightly. A breeze brushes over my face, and it feels like heaven. I glance at the evening sky, and a deep ache pulls at my chest. Why does the whole world look beautiful?

A relationship with her wouldn't last, even if we both fell in love. It would all fade away eventually, and then I would have nothing left.

Oh God, what am I going to do?

NINE

Livvy

WHAT JUST HAPPENED?

Cole had looked bewildered, which I guess is reasonable considering how much I've insisted over the years that I would only date another Christian. Could that have prevented him from being with me all this time?

Many years ago, when I was so devout that I couldn't understand how anyone wouldn't want to be a Christian, it seemed like only a small barrier. It seemed that if he really liked me, he would come to church with me. He would at least ask me to share my faith with him, because that's what you do when you're interested in someone you really like. It was so simple.

I was so selfish and naive. I expected him to change his whole worldview when I wasn't willing to compromise my beliefs in any way.

I hadn't thought about any of this for a long time. Over the last few months, in an effort to squash the delusional hope I've harbored for years, I've told myself over and over again that he doesn't want me. He doesn't touch me. He doesn't flirt with me. He loves me as a platonic friend, and he always will.

It takes me a moment to find Travis in the crowd. He's sitting in the exact spot I left him. I take a deep breath to steel myself before heading in his direction. After whatever just happened outside, my first instinct is to forget all about my plans for tonight and spend the evening with Cole, but I can't do that. That's what the old me would do. I always drop everything for him, and I still don't even know what his reaction was about. He got skittish when I asked him about it.

I form a smile on my face as I approach Travis. When I set a hand on his shoulder, he turns to me and grins widely like he's delighted to see me.

Maybe he isn't so bad.

"Do you know where Mari is?" I ask.

"I think she's still on the dance floor." He sets his hand on my shoulder and guides me to the bar stool next to his. "I just ordered something for you. I think you're going to like it."

I glance at the wooden counter. "What happened to my drink?"

"I downed it after you left with Cole."

"Oh..."

"I could tell you didn't like it but were too nice to tell me."

I lick my lips, lifting a hand and tucking a strand of hair behind my ear. "It was just a little strong."

The bartender appears and places three small glasses in front of Travis. My eyes widen. "Shots? Is one of these for me?"

Travis grins. "They're all for you. It's the perfect solution. You can get drunk without having to taste the alcohol."

"*All* for me? That's a lot to drink."

"You'll be fine." He leans in close, his breath brushing over my face as he says, "I don't know why Cole's being so weird about you drinking when he passed out in my bathroom the last time we went out drinking. He's freaking you out for no reason. Even if you get drunk fast, you'll be fine. Trust me."

I take a deep breath and glance down at the shots. Even if I do get sick, who cares? Both Cole and Mari have gotten so drunk that they've puked, and that didn't stop them from going out and partying again. Besides, this is supposed to be an adventure. I should be going all out.

When I reach out and grab one of the shots, Travis pats my back. "Yes!"

I clench my fingers around the glass and lift it to my mouth. Nervousness flutters through me, but with it is a mixture of exhilaration. I throw the shot back into my mouth the same way I've seen other people do it, and thankfully, only a slight burn trails down my throat.

"That's my girl!" Travis claps.

"Livvy!" I twist around and see Mari and Zac making their way through the crowd. "Did you really just take a shot?"

I smile widely. "It burned, and I loved it!"

"Isn't she so cute?" Travis wraps his arms around me and pulls my back against his chest. "It was a Lemon Drop too. A Lemon Drop burned her throat."

I don't know what a Lemon Drop is, but I can tell he's making fun of me, and I don't care. For the first time, I'm living like a regular college student.

He presses a kiss against my cheek. "You should hurry up and get another shot down before your nanny comes back."

I wince. "Another one? I don't even feel this one yet."

He laughs. "You'll be fine."

My gaze darts to Mari. "Do you think I should take another one?"

"It's up to you. You said you wanted to go all out, and you

have plenty of people here to take care of you." Her smile grows cheeky. "You have one person who will take extra good care of you if you get too drunk."

"Yeah, but he'll be mad." I glance around the area. "He told me I should only have one drink an hour."

"I think you should do it while he's not looking," Zac says. "But don't tell him I said that."

"Dude!" Travis shouts. "Cole needs to chill the fuck out. Why is he like this with her? She shouldn't be scared to take shots." He looks at me. "Don't let him get into your head. Do what you want to do."

Mari leans forward, raising her voice over the noise of the crowd. "I agree with him. I love Cole to death, but sometimes he acts like if he touches you too hard, you'll shatter. And the whole problem is that *you're* scared you might shatter."

She's right. She's absolutely right. And the biggest problem of all is that I let Cole treat me like I might shatter because I was trained to let men take care of me.

That has to stop. I have to take care of myself.

I grab another one of the shots and throw it back. The cheers of the others register at the back of my mind, but I have to stay focused if I'm going to get through this. After inwardly plugging my nose, I lift the next shot, not wanting to give my brain time to register disgust. Within seconds, the burning liquid is trailing down my throat.

"Holy shit!" Mari shouts. "I can't believe you actually did that."

Exhilaration courses through my veins. I can't believe I did it either. I turn to Mari, beaming. "I'm aging fast tonight. You had your first shot at what... Sixteen? Seventeen?"

"Fifteen."

I smile, surprised that I don't feel even the slightest pang of resentment she never told me about it. It's probably because she knew I would have been disappointed in her. It used to bother me when these little facts slipped out over the years as she grew more comfortable opening up to me, but not anymore.

"So I just turned fifteen," I say. "Hopefully, by the end of the night—"

"What was that?" Cole's deep, rumbly voice sends a shiver down my spine. When I turn around, all the bewilderment in his eyes is gone. He's glaring at Travis like he's ready to punch him.

Goodness, I need to defuse this. I can't let them fight over me again.

I smile at Cole as warmth drifts over my body like a low morning tide. Is this the alcohol? It feels lovely.

"I just took two shots back-to-back," I say, "and it was amazing."

When I giggle, Cole's scowl grows. "I was out there for ten minutes at the most. Why do you look drunk already?"

My gaze snaps to Travis. "Could they have kicked in that fast?"

He shakes his head. "You're probably feeling that first shot."

"That first shot?" Cole is all but yelling now. "Are you telling me she's had three shots in the amount of time I was outside? Fuck. I never should have left her alone for even a minute." He looks at Mari and Zac. "Where were you guys?"

Mari crosses her arms over her chest. "What Livvy drinks is entirely up to her. Calm down, Daddy."

He shakes his head, his jaw tightening.

"It's okay, Cole." Zac sets his hand on his shoulder and gives it a squeeze. "Just let her have fun."

"She's five foot nothing!" He gestures over me. "She's going to start stumbling around in a couple of minutes."

"So what if I do? Right now, I just want to dance!" I lift my hands in the air and sway to the music, gyrating my hips in a way I've only ever done in front of Mari and Vanessa.

Oh man, this feels good. Somehow, my limbs are looser and my hips are more fluid. I glance at Travis, gesturing toward the dance floor. "Let's go!"

He grins as he grabs me by the waist. I twist around to give Cole a reassuring smile, but his grim expression freezes my face. His anger is mixed with something else... Desolation, maybe, like I'm being pulled away for good, and he'll never be able to reach me.

"Don't get pregnant!" Zac shouts, and Cole's expression grows even darker.

Travis laughs and pulls me onto the dance floor. I sway my hips to the beat. Just as I find a rhythm I like, he pulls my body against his. He presses his hips into mine while we dance. It's amazing that I don't want to pull back.

Has alcohol really squashed all of my fear?

I test it by stepping away from Travis and turning my back to him. I peak over my shoulder while I whirl my hips. When he sends an appreciative look over my body, I laugh. My butt is jiggling, and I don't even care.

His warm hands touch my bare shoulders, and he yanks my back against his chest. "Oh man, you're fun when you're drunk."

I smile as I lean back. His body is warm and hard, just like Cole's was last night. That kiss. The way he held me tightly and pressed his hips into my belly, like he needed more. I needed more too.

His warm hand drifts down my side, and heat pools in my belly. Yes. This is what I need. Something soft and wet presses against my neck, and I hum.

When I open my eyes, Cole's face immediately comes into

view. Why is he so far away? His body is utterly still, and his expression is blank, like he's shocked.

"Do you like that?" Travis's voice vibrates in my ear, and a jolt of alarm punctures my heavy daze. How did I forget about Travis? When I twist around to look at his face, my stomach does an unpleasant little turn. There are two of him. There are actually two of him, like I've seen in movies. I blink hard, and when I open my eyes, the images are fused, but only for a moment, and then they split into two again.

This isn't good.

"Yeah, I liked that," I say, hoping to hide my nervousness.

He smiles and pulls me close, and the warmth of his body eases some of my anxiety, but the feeling is short lived.

Travis pulls away from me so suddenly that I almost lose my balance. A firm grip on my arm pulls me upright.

"What the fuck?" Travis shouts.

"She's not going anywhere near you," Cole grits out. "I'm taking her home."

My sluggish confusion quickly shifts into indignation. "I'm not going home now. The night's barely started."

When Cole turns to me, his jaw is set, but his eyes are softer than they were a moment ago. "I've been watching you for the last half hour. You're really drunk, Liv. Too drunk."

I wrinkle my nose. "Half hour? I've only been dancing for, like, two minutes."

"Trust me, it's been half an hour, and he's been getting handsier every second." His expression grows hard as his gaze shifts to Travis.

"Dude, chill the fuck out. I didn't do anything she didn't want me to do."

I'm about to open my mouth to agree with him when nausea overtakes me suddenly. I turn around and rush in the direction of the door. The mugginess of the warm bodies around me makes bile rise at the back of my throat. I don't make it far before a pair of strong hands grip my waist.

"I've got you."

Cole's voice sends a rush of warmth through me, momentarily distracting me from my sickness. He cuts through the crowd with such force that most people step away to let him through.

As soon as we make it outside, I inhale a deep breath of ocean air, and it instantly calms the stirring in my gut.

"Are you okay?" His voice is gentle.

"I'm fine." At least I have the wherewithal to recognize that my words aren't quite precise.

"Sweetheart, you're wasted. If you're not feeling good, just tell me."

"I'm a little dizzy. I think the shots finally fully hit me."

When he tightens his grip on my waist and pulls my back against his chest, electricity shoots into my gut. "What can I get for you?"

I relax into his warmth. "Let's go to another bar. Just the two of us."

He jerks back. "No, I'm taking you home. You've had way too much."

"We can't leave Mariana."

"She'll be fine. Zac already promised to get her home safe."

I frown. "I want to dance more."

"That's the alcohol talking. If I let you on a dance floor, you're going to fall over."

I twist around in his grip so that I can stare up into his eyes. "Then dance with me. You can hold me up."

Something flashes in his eyes, but then he looks away. "No. We'll try this again another night. Come to my place now so you can rest before I take you home. That way you don't have to worry about your parents seeing you drunk."

Goodness, resting at his place sounds so good. He'll probably rub my back until I fall asleep, like the time I got sick at his apartment. He's so caring.

But also incredibly domineering.

I lift my chin. "I want to dance more."

He looks like he's fighting an eye roll. "You're drunk."

"I am drunk, and I want to dance."

Now he rolls his eyes in earnest. "Alright. Obviously, you're even drunker than I thought." His hold on my waist tightens, and I shriek as he lifts me into his arms and cradles me against his chest. He carries me down the sidewalk toward his car. After opening the passenger door, he sets me gently inside.

He crouches down, poking his head into the car. "I'm going inside to get your purse. I won't be gone more than a minute. Don't stumble off anywhere, Angel."

He says it with a smile because he doesn't think there's a chance in hell I'd actually leave. I always do as he says. I've never had a reason not to.

Do I have a reason now, or do I just feel like I do because I'm drunk?

There's something strangely exhilarating about the thought of Cole coming out of that bar and finding me gone after he ordered me to stay in here.

As soon as his back disappears inside, I leap from my seat and run down the sidewalk. I throw my head back and lift my arms high in the air. I'm so lightheaded and buoyant, I could drift into the sky like a helium balloon.

Eventually, I slow my pace, because although drunkenness might feel like magic at the moment, it doesn't seem to have given me magical stamina. While I catch my breath, I realize I'm standing in front of the Tiki bar that Mari had planned on taking me to tonight.

My stomach flips as I walk inside. Here I am at a bar alone

after ditching my domineering best friend who acts like a jealous boyfriend but doesn't want to have sex with me.

I'm standing up for myself.

I glance around the misty bar, unsure of where to go next. I don't want another drink, and there isn't a dance floor in here. I'm just about ready to turn around and search for another bar when a guy waves me over to a group of people sitting in the back corner. I don't hesitate to walk in their direction, and I'm amazed anew at the effectiveness of alcohol in taking away my fear.

Only the faintest pang of regret punctures my boozy haze. Cole is going to be worried when he finds me gone.

How long have I been gone?

As I get closer to the group, the mist clears, and their images grow sharper. Goodness, it's all guys.

"I know you," a blond guy says, his gaze roaming my body. "You go to UCSB, right? Where have I seen you before?"

"I'm not sure..." I scan his face. "You don't look familiar."

He shrugs. "Oh, well. Why don't you come over here so we can get to know each other?"

When he pats his thigh, my mouth drops open. Does he really expect me to sit on his lap when I don't even know him? Distantly, I recognize that the other guys are laughing.

"Why do you have to be so fucking creepy?" one of them says before looking at me. "Don't do it, beautiful. Come sit next to me instead."

"There's no room." The blond guy smiles at me. "You'll be way more comfortable on my lap."

"The fuck she will." Cole's booming voice is like a soft blanket, even though I know he's furious with me.

"Oh shit!" the blond guy says, and all the others start laughing. "I'm so sorry, man. She didn't say she has a boyfriend."

Cole ignores him and turns to me. His blazing eyes send a

chill down my spine. I've never seen him look so angry. "You can either walk out with me now, or I'm carrying you."

I lower my gaze to the floor. "I'll go with you."

"Good choice." He grabs my hand and squeezes it tightly. My stomach lurches as he pulls me through the bar. His usual athletic grace is gone. His posture is so rigid he looks like he might snap in two.

When we make it outside, he lets go of my hand and turns to me. "What the fuck has gotten into you?"

Oh Jesus, he's never cursed at me before. He's never spoken to me with so much contempt. With effort, I raise my chin and hold his stare, though my eyes are starting to prickle.

"I told you I want to stay out, and you didn't listen to me." My voice doesn't sound nearly as firm as I want.

His jaw clenches. "I can't believe you just did that. I never would have expected it of you in a million years, even drunk."

I take a deep breath to keep my lips from quivering. "I wanted an adventure."

"An adventure," he scoffs. "You ran off in the middle of the night with drunk people everywhere when *you* can barely stand up straight. You don't even have your phone on you, so I had no way of finding you. I was lucky I walked in there."

"I'm sorry." My voice is small.

He shakes his head. "This is so unlike you. I wasn't even totally sure you ran off. I thought maybe someone kidnapped you."

"I'm so sorry."

"You're not forgiven." He steps back and takes a deep, shaky breath, setting his hand at the center of his chest. "My heart is still pounding. I was *so* worried."

He doesn't sound angry now, and it's the final straw. I lose what's left of my flimsy drunken self-control. The first tear rolls down my cheek, and I can't stop my face from scrunching up.

When his eyes grow huge, I turn away, unable to bear the humiliation. "Just give me a second."

I keep my gaze fixed on the concrete as I take a few steps. The cold, misty wind brushing over my hot cheeks is a momentary relief. "I won't go far, I promise."

"Livvy, oh my God." His voice has returned to its usual gentleness, but it doesn't lessen my shame.

I hate being so soft. It's so humiliating. Even when I try to be adventurous, I'm still weak and timid.

Maybe I can't blame my upbringing for my subservience. Maybe I made the ideal obedient Christian girl because I was born this way, and nothing I do will ever change that.

When I'm yanked against a hard chest, I release the breath I was holding.

"I'm so sorry," he says. "I can't believe I made you cry. I'm an asshole. I shouldn't have gotten so mad at you when you're drunk. It was my fault for leaving you alone."

His anger would be easier to bear than his tenderness in my fragile mood. In the end, I can't help but bury my head against his chest and cry. My heaving sobs only make my humiliation that much more acute.

"Oh God, Livvy, you're killing me right now. I'm so sorry."

"It's okay. I'm just stupidly sensitive." My voice is muffled against his chest, and he squeezes me so tightly that, for a moment, I can't take a breath.

"Aww, sweetheart, I know you're sensitive, and it's okay. I can't believe I just yelled at you. What the fuck is wrong with me?"

"You're a natural leader." My stomach lurches. "And I'm a natural follower."

"A leader," he scoffs. "I've been acting like a fucking dictator with you tonight." He presses his cheek against my head. "And you're not a follower. You're just considerate, and

I've only been thinking about myself. I promise to try harder. You want to stay out and drink more? I'll keep you safe."

"No, I want to go home, and you were being kind of a dictator, but not about this. I'd be so mad at you if you made me worried on purpose, but you wouldn't cry like a baby about it. I wish I wasn't so sensitive. I always cry when people get mad at me..." Another wave of humiliation washes over me, and I sob even harder.

He brushes his lips over the top of my head, sending tingles into my scalp. Goodness, he's touched me more in the past twenty-four hours than he has during our whole friendship.

It feels so good.

"It's okay. You don't have to be embarrassed for being sensitive. I love that about you."

Hearing the word love on his lips nearly breaks me. My body becomes a deadweight in his arms, but he doesn't seem to mind.

"I hate it. It makes me weak."

"No, it doesn't." His voice is firm. "You're compassionate and in tune with other people's emotions. Those are strengths."

I laugh humorlessly, but it sounds more like a sob. "I'm only compassionate because it makes me feel terrible to be any other way. I feel terrible when I hurt or disappoint people. It's not real compassion. It's fear."

He squeezes me tightly. "Livvy, that's silly. Most people are too busy thinking about themselves to care about whether they've hurt or disappointed people. Don't discount your kindness just because it comes naturally to you."

"But it isn't *just* compassion. I'm a huge pushover and people pleaser."

I lift my head and look into his deep brown eyes. They're heavy-lidded and tender, and only belatedly do I realize that his warm fingers are caressing the skin around my ear. Liquid heat fills my belly in a rush.

"What?" His voice is thick.

I can't allow myself to be this way anymore. I need to be assertive. I need to ask for what I want as if I'm worthy of it.

"I'm asking you again to take my virginity, and I want you to answer me this time. If you don't want to do it, just tell me."

Cole

MY ARMS ARE AROUND HER, and the pads of my fingers are brushing against the soft skin around her ears. Fuck. What am I doing? How did I forget myself?

I can't think when I'm close to her like this, and I need time to think. I can't answer her now.

Not after the bomb she dropped earlier tonight. Having sex with her would mean so much more than what I thought when she first made her proposal.

It could be the beginning of something.

Fuck, my chest constricts tightly again. I could be with her. She could be mine.

But it would only be temporary.

I set my hands on her shoulders and go to gently push her away, but she holds me tightly. "We can't talk about this now," I say. "Not while you're drunk."

"If you're not attracted to me, just say it."

I want to throw my head back and laugh. How is she so wise about certain things and yet absurdly naive about others?

"Of course I'm attracted to you. You're a beautiful girl."

Her brow furrows. "I don't think that means anything. You're just trying not to hurt my feelings. I've seen you with women you want. You're touchy. You can't keep your hands off them, and you never touch me. At least, not normally."

She runs her nails up the back of my neck, and I groan. I need to pull away from her, but I can't bring myself to do it.

"I like touching you," I say, "but I've always respected you too much—"

"Gross!" She wrinkles her nose.

I frown. "It's gross that I respect you?"

"It's gross that you think respecting me means keeping your hands off me, especially when I want your touch."

Her hands glide down my back and she leans into me, humming as she nuzzles my chest with her nose. "You smell so good."

My whole body grows stiff. "What are you doing?"

"I'm hugging you." The sound is muffled against my shirt. "I think liking someone's smell is a sign you really want them, don't you? I've thought so many guys were good-looking over the years, but none of them have smelled as good as you. Do you like the way I smell, too?"

As if she cast a spell, her wonderful scent washes over me. I do love the way she smells, and I'm certain I would love the way she tastes too.

Fuck.

I hold my whole body rigid, resisting the urge to groan at the softness of her tits as they press against my chest. "You're drunk. You don't know what you're saying."

"I am drunk, but I know what I'm saying. Do you want me or not? Just be honest."

Oh God. She's killing me. And even her innocent mind probably knows it. There's no way she could be pressed up against me like this without feeling evidence of how turned on I am. My rock-hard dick is probably digging into her skin through that flimsy dress.

She looks up at me and smiles—a sultry quirk of her lips that's completely unlike the Livvy I know. "Do you like it when I do this?" She moves her hips slightly forward. It's a small motion—not even really a thrust—and yet it sets me on fire. I know I need to push her away, but my arms feel like they're glued to her, like they have a will of their own.

"You did that to me when we kissed, and it made me—" she lowers her voice, "—wet."

"Oh fuck, Livvy." My voice is a rasp. "Please stop. I'm begging you."

"Okay." Her smile grows bolder as she drops her arms at her side. "Now you're the one touching me. Why don't you stop?"

My groan is so loud it's almost a growl. I lift my hands and set them on her cheek, forcing her to look at me. "I cannot have this conversation with you right now. You're drunk, and I need to think. This is not something I can decide on a horny impulse. Your friendship means more to me than any—"

I'm startled when she jerks away from me. "If I hear how much our friendship means to you one more time, I think I might throw up."

I scowl. "What the fuck does that mean?"

When she whips around, her eyes are blazing. "It means I'm sick of excuses. I'm not asking you to give up our friendship."

I open my mouth and close it. "You don't know how it might—"

"No, I don't know." She sets her hands on her hips. "I don't know if it will change things between us because I'm not God, but I do know that the door is closing. I'm not going to sit around and wait forever for you to decide. I'm giving you three days."

"Three days? Are you fucking kidding me? This is a big deal. It's not something I can decide quickly."

Her jaw hardens as she shrugs. "You've known me for five years. If three days isn't enough for you to decide if you want to have sex with me, I think that's a pretty good sign you don't."

I grit my teeth, struggling for control. "You already know that I want you. You felt my cock pressing into you when you hugged me."

When her eyes grow hesitant, I smile darkly. For all her drunken boldness, she has no idea what she's doing or who she's dealing with. Words like "cock" terrify her. She only thinks she wants this because she doesn't know what she's asking for.

If I showed her the full extent of my desire for her, she would run away.

"This is about much more than sex, but if you need to set a deadline, I'll respect it. Just know that I'm going to err on the side of caution. If I haven't made a decision by then, the answer will be no."

When her face falls, I want to reach out and hold her, but I can't touch her again. Instead, I soften my voice. "Come on. It's only ten now. Let's hurry back to my place so you can get a good nap in before I take you home."

LIVVY

"DRUNKEN ANGEL, it's time to wake up." The soft voice curls through my insides, pulling me from the darkness. Big, warm fingers brush my cheek. When the world comes into focus, Cole's handsome face is in my view, smiling tenderly. Goodness, where am I?

As I stare at him, memories drizzle back in. On the car ride home from the bar, I got dizzy. Cole told me to lie back in my seat and shut my eyes. I think he rubbed my arm. But what happened before that? Oh, that's right. The conversation on the sidewalk.

Jesus, help me, I threw myself at him.

When I sit up suddenly, he sets his hands on my shoulders and gives them a squeeze. "It's okay. It's only midnight."

"I'm not worried about that." I glance around the room, trying to collect my scattered thoughts. My gaze settles at the wet spot on his pillow, and I wrinkle my nose. "Oh no, I drooled on your pillow."

He laughs softly. "You sleep with your mouth open."

When I grab the pillow and start yanking down the case, he sets his hand on mine. "A little bit of spit isn't going to kill me."

"It's gross."

"Most people's spit is gross. Yours isn't."

My gaze snaps to his face, and he's smiling faintly. "Does that weird you out? If it does, I'm probably not the guy to take your virginity."

I stare at him for a moment. "Do you really not think my spit is gross?"

He leans forward, stopping when his face is a few inches from mine. The warmth of his skin radiates from him, and that's when it finally settles over me that I'm lying in a bed, and he's sitting on the side of it. Close. Close enough that I could pull him in.

"Nothing about you is gross," he says.

Our gazes hold for a moment, and something flashes in his eyes, something that looks like defiance. "I could bury my head between your legs and never come out."

He watches me for a moment, and then he smiles, his eyelids growing lazy. He looks like he wants to laugh at me.

"I would lick every part of you if I could. I mean it when I say *every* part. Not just your pussy."

His words don't compute at first. Where else could he lick me? When it dawns on me what he might mean, a flaming heat washes from my scalp to my chest. "Are you talking about... Would you lick my...?"

"Your ass? Yeah, that's what I'm talking about. And I wouldn't just lick it once. I could lick it for days."

Goodness, I knew people did things like that, but it always seemed like an abstract concept. I never thought people I knew did it, or that someone would want to do it to me. And not just someone. Cole. My Cole.

When he laughs, I realize my eyes must be popping out of my skull, but I'm not weirded out. His words, though shocking, make heat curl in my belly.

"This is what I was trying to explain to you when you first asked me if I could do this. Not everyone likes the same things, and I know the things I like would scare you. You probably want a sweet, romantic first time with candles and music in the background. You'd want someone to be really slow and restrained with you, and I'd definitely try..." His eyes grow molten. "But I don't know if I could." His voice is deep and dark. "I've wanted you for five years. When you first told me you were planning to stay pure, all I could think was...how much I wanted to make you dirty."

My stomach flips so hard I'm surprised I don't hunch over. "Really?"

"Yep. Is that blasphemy?"

"No." My voice is small. "I think I'd like it if you made me dirty."

"You *think*." His devilish smile tells me he doesn't quite believe me. He lifts a hand and brushes a strand of hair behind my ear. "Think about it more over the next three days. I will too. Remember that it won't be just sex. Not between you and me."

Of course it won't. Not when I love him from the pit of my soul.

He runs his fingers down my neck before settling his hand on my shoulder. "We shouldn't be around each other while we think. I don't even think we should text."

My stomach plummets. He's never ever asked for time away from me. Usually, he's so demanding of my time. He practically called dibs on me during holiday breaks. He must really be tormented by this decision.

"I don't like it either," he says, caressing my shoulder with his thumb. "But it's hard for me to think clearly about this when I'm around you, and this is a big deal to me. *You're* a big deal to me."

I nod slowly, unable to speak. He leans forward, hesitating for only the briefest moment before pressing his lips softly against mine.

TEN

Cole

I STRETCH my arms and legs out, relishing the softness of my bed. I've been awake for a while now, but I haven't wanted to move. She hasn't left my mind for even a second since I dropped her off last night.

She was sleeping here. Right where I am.

I can't seem to stop thinking about the fact that she could be sleeping here now. If I had agreed two days ago, her head could've been resting on the pillow next to mine.

No. She wouldn't be on the pillow next to mine, because I'd have her in my arms. I'd be able to touch her as much as I want. I wouldn't have to hold myself back like I did last night, periodically peeking in the room, telling myself I was checking on her but really just wanting to look at her while she slept in my bed.

She'd be mine. I'd have just fucked her, and every curve of her body would already be familiar to me.

Oh, fuck.

I'm going to do it.

Somehow, all of my reservations disappeared during the night. I know they're there deep down, prickling at the back of my consciousness, but I hardly even feel their effects anymore. Euphoria is drowning out all of my anxiety.

In three days, I'll have her.

A soft knock sounds on my front door, and a prickle of foreboding punctures through my elation. That was my mom's knock, and she never disturbs me in the morning after I've been out with my friends. Not this early.

When I open the door, her expression is grim. She looks over my shoulder into my living room. "Do you have a lady friend over?"

"No." I frown. "Why, what's up?"

"I just wanted you to know I'm heading out for an overnight trip with Maddy and Mason. We're going to the Tahoe cabin. It'll just be you and your dad here."

"Okay. That's fine—"

"I didn't plan it. I decided this morning. Your dad shattered the living room window last night. The big one over the couch."

I stare at her dumbly. "What happened?"

My apprehension grows when she slips past me and walks inside the guesthouse instead of answering. After sitting down on the couch, she stares at me steadily. "He was drinking last night and threw something at it."

A shiver rolls down my back. "What the fuck? Why would he do that?"

She exhales heavily. "He told me he's scheduled an appointment with a marriage counselor. He practically ordered me to go with him, but I told him I won't. It's too late for that— for me, at least. I was actually sort of proud of myself, because I usually have a hard time standing my ground with him. But then—" her voice grows hushed, "—he started crying. Sobbing is probably a better description. I couldn't believe it. I haven't seen your dad cry since your grandpa passed away, and it was nothing like this..." She looks away from me. "I'm sorry. I shouldn't be telling you this. I was just so surprised."

"Me too," I say absently, my head swimming.

Why would he be so upset? He had to know this day was coming.

"Anyway." She stands up from the couch. "I have to get Maddy and Mason out of here. They were so confused last night when the alarm went off. I haven't told them about the divorce yet, but I think they sense that something is wrong, and I have a feeling that if your dad is upset enough to throw a candle at the window, he's not going—"

"He threw a candle at the window?"

She nods slowly. "I found it when I was cleaning up the glass."

"That glass is like two inches thick. He was able to shatter the whole thing with a candle?"

"It was one of the jar candles from my knitting room."

What the fuck was he doing in her knitting room? It's her sanctuary. I even feel like I have to talk quietly when I'm in there, and I only ever disturb her there when I absolutely need something. I haven't seen my dad in there in years.

"Don't look so skeptical." My mom smiles faintly. "His fastball was even better than yours at one time."

His fastball. Oh God. I don't want to think about baseball and my dad. It used to be such a big part of my life. Our father-son trips to Arizona for the Dodger's spring training were some of the happiest memories of my childhood. Glendale, with its bluish sunlight and unnaturally warm air, was like a strange desert planet compared to Santa Barbara. My dad and I would go to that outdoor German brat house in Scottsdale after the games. He would sneak me sips of his spicy beer when the servers weren't looking, and I would pretend like it wasn't disgusting. We would talk for hours. Not about anything earth-shattering—mostly just baseball. But that time with him was everything to me.

Somehow, those memories are still bright and warm. Somehow, catching him with that woman didn't cast a pall over those moments, only everything else.

Inexplicably, mist rises to my eyes, and my chest starts to ache. I'm gripped with a powerful longing for the life I had before, when I thought my dad was a different person. When I thought my parents had a different marriage.

I lived in a dream world of my own making. The signs were there. I was just too self-absorbed to see them. My dad and mom hardly talked to each other, and there was a sadness to my mom during quiet moments.

Her smile fades. "Sorry. I know there's nothing funny about this."

"No, Mom, it's okay. I'm just...processing it all." I frown. "What was he doing with a candle from your knitting room?"

"I don't know." She sounds as perplexed as I am. "He went in there after our argument about the marriage counselor. He was acting very strange, but I guess it's understandable. Divorce is really hard, even for people in unhealthy marriages. He's still not awake, and you know your dad never sleeps in. He must have been very drunk last night. I'm not sure if he even knows he broke the window. He wasn't there by the time I made it downstairs. He passed out in one of the guest rooms, and I didn't feel like confronting him." She shakes her head. "The glass was everywhere. All over the couch and the floor and the back patio."

God, he's a piece of shit. Breaking a window in the middle of the night and leaving my mom to clean up the mess. What a perfect metaphor for their marriage.

"Honey, I know all of this must be hard for you, even at your age."

"I'm fine, Mom."

She gives me a wary look. "Cole, you can talk to me. I know it's uncomfortable, but you can. It's not going to hurt me."

"There's nothing to talk about. You already...know everything. At least the important part—that he's a cheater."

"I don't want to talk about the things he's done. I mean we can talk about how you feel."

I avert my gaze from hers. She's done this a few times before, prompted me to share my feelings with her. How could she think I'd be that selfish and vent to her about my daddy issues when she's the one most affected by his behavior?

"Every time I ask you how you're feeling, you get so closed off. You say you're fine, but I can see that you're not. You were different after that trip to Arizona. Whatever you saw must have..." She shakes her head. "I wish I had gotten you counseling. I wish I had just made you go."

"There was no way you could have made me, and he's not worth counseling."

She purses her lips primly, looking like she wants to roll her eyes. "I think the point is that you're worth counseling. But what I'm trying to say is that I'm okay. You can talk to me. I'm not going to crumble. My priority is you and your brother and sister. If you ever want to talk, I'm here."

She walks toward the door. After setting her hand on the knob, she turns to me. "I think you need to stay out of your dad's way this weekend. No matter how angry you are with him, it'll be hard for you to see him the way he is right now. He's not himself."

I wave a hand. "I'll be fine."

She sighs. "It would mean a lot to me if you promise to stay out of his way. Maybe get out of the house today. Go for a hike."

"If it'll make you feel better, I will."

She smiles warmly before walking out the door. As soon as the sound of her footsteps fade, I leap up from the couch, running frantic hands through my hair as I head into my bedroom.

I need Livvy. She'll be able to make sense of all this. After I make it to my bedside table and grab my phone, my hand freezes.

Fuck.

I'm not supposed to see her for three days. By my own request.

I pull up Zac's name instead, and he picks up on the first ring. "If you're calling instead of texting, something is wrong. What happened?"

I sigh heavily. "It's a long story, and I don't feel like going into it right now, but it involves my cheating asshole dad. As usual."

"Aww shit, dude. Is your mom okay?"

"I don't know. It's always hard for me to tell with her, but my dad is not doing okay, which is...weird."

"Aww man, I'm sorry. Do you want to come hang out?"

"Yeah, I need to get out of my house. Any chance you want to go for a hike?"

"Um..." He laughs softly. "I mean, I'm hungover as fuck, so no, but I will if you really want me to."

"Yes, I do. Get your lazy ass out of bed. I'll bring weed for your hangover."

"Well, in that case... Actually, why don't we invite Mari and Livvy? Livvy told me she wants to try weed for the first time."

I grit my teeth. "I can't invite Livvy. We have some...stuff we're trying to figure out right now. With our friendship."

"Yeah, Mari told me what she asked you to do."

I roll my eyes. "Of course she did."

"Why is this even an issue? I thought you'd jump at the opportunity. You're obviously obsessed with her. You can't bull-shit me about this. I know you."

I grit my teeth, not wanting to get into it with him. "My relationship with her is complicated."

"If you say it is. Well, if you aren't going to do it, Travis is trying to make a move. He told me he's going to ask her to go to his parents' church with him tomorrow."

Heat breaks out over my skin. "What the fuck?"

"Calm down." He sounds like he's repressing laughter. "It's the only in he has with her, and it's a pretty low move. I'm not sure if God exists, but if he does, I think he'll probably strike people down for using church to get pussy. Isn't that blasphemy?"

My skin tingles when a memory surfaces. The shrill sound of that pastor's voice on Sunday mornings when I was hungover. The itching urge to get out of that dim auditorium and back into the sunlight. For a year, I went to church for kind of the same reason.

"Why do you act like this if you don't want her?" he asks. "You can't do it forever. Eventually, you're going to have to either be with her or get out of the way."

I shut my eyes tightly. "I don't want to talk about this right now. I have too much going on in my life."

He sighs. "Alright fine. I'll see you in a bit. I want to fucking die right now, so don't be mad if I lag on our hike."

"Wait."

I take a deep breath, unable to believe what I'm about to do, but the thought of her with another guy makes me want to burst out of my skin. Apparently, I'm so primitive that I can't even take three days to make sure I'm not making the worst mistake of my life.

"Don't worry about the hike," I say in a rush. "I think I'm going to ask Livvy instead."

He laughs. "Good choice."

As soon as we hang up, I pull up her name and type out a text. An exultant wave washes over me after I press send, and my heart starts to pound like a drum.

In possibly a matter of hours, she'll be mine.

ELEVEN

Livvy

AS I MAKE my sluggish way into the kitchen, I catch sight of Vanessa sitting in the living room watching TV. She turns to me, and I brace myself for her judgment.

"Are you just now waking up?" Her voice is full of disbelief. "You really did get drunk, huh?"

As I stand on my toes to grab a mug from the cupboard, a sharp pain shoots into my head, making me wince. "Yes, and I don't think I'll do it again for a while. I feel like death."

"I never thought you would get that drunk in the first place. I can't believe you have a hangover."

"I'm long overdue for it. I've been to plenty of parties as the designated driver. It was nice being able to actually have fun for a change."

She stands up from the couch and walks into the kitchen. "Did it make you feel like a bold, adventurous woman?"

Her sarcasm makes me flinch. I might have been able to

deal with it if I weren't hungover, but my nerves are raw. I frown at her. "I know it's hard for you that I'm changing, but I still expect you to respect my choices, even if you don't understand them. You don't think purity culture is toxic and want to save yourself for your husband, and on your wedding day—assuming your beliefs stay the same until then—I'm going to tell you how proud I am of you for sticking with your convictions. I trust you to do what's right for you, and I need you to do the same for me, Ness. Even if you don't like it. Even if it scares you."

Her adorable little face scrunches inward, and she starts to cry. My heart clenches, and I rush over to her and wrap my arms around her shoulders. "Oh, honey, I didn't mean to be so harsh."

"I'm just tired." She turns her head away from me, and a small smile rises to my lips even as my chest aches for her.

"Why are you upset?"

"I just want my old sister back."

"I'm still your old sister. I haven't changed all that much."

"Yes, you have." She jerks away from me. "You're doing all kinds of things you never would have done even a few months ago. Cole is going to fall in love with you now that he can have sex with you, and you're going to get married and become an atheist like him. You're going to think I'm stupid and anti-intellectual for my beliefs, and you'll never respect me again. I'll never be able to talk about my life with anyone."

I suck in my lips to fight a smile. Oh goodness, she's so sweet. I would have felt the exact same way in her place—so scared and uncertain over something that really has nothing to do with me. "I will always be the old Livvy when it comes to you. You can always talk about your life with me, and I'll never think you're stupid or anti-intellectual. And there's no way I'll become an atheist. I love Jesus way too much."

"I'm scared that isn't true," she says, her voice choked. "I'm scared you're going to replace Jesus with Cole."

I squeeze her shoulders. "Honey, Cole and I aren't even together. He doesn't even know if he wants to take my virginity. And even if he does, even if we get together, I won't allow myself to make him my entire world. I don't think it was healthy when I made Jesus my entire world. I have too many other things in my life I love to give all of myself to one person. You're one of those things. How could you ever think I would sacrifice my relationship with you for a man?"

Her face is still averted from mine, and she lifts a hand to wipe tears from under her eyes. "I just don't want you to look down on me."

"I never will. How could I? I'd be a total hypocrite. At one time, I believed all the same things you do now, and I was much more self-righteous about it than you are. And besides that, I love you more than anything."

Footsteps sound down the stairs, and she and I both look up. A few seconds later, my dad walks into the kitchen with a stern frown on his face. He looks at Vanessa. "I need to talk to your sister."

"Dad," I say, "we're kind of having a moment right now."

His eyes grow hard. "I need to talk to you."

"I'm fine," Vanessa says. "We can talk later."

"No." I shoot her a meaningful look. "I want you here."

Understanding dawns in her eyes.

I look at my dad. "You may want to talk to me alone, but I want Vanessa here while you lecture me about getting drunk last night."

He lets out a forceful breath. "She's seventeen, and this conversation is not for her."

"She'll legally be an adult in a few weeks, and I need her support."

He crosses his arms over his chest. "You need her support because you know you're sinning."

I raise my chin. "It's not your place to police my faith."

"Then I think you need to give your pastor a call. See what he says."

"Since I'm currently without a pastor, I have no one to call. But this is exactly why I left First Covenant. I need a pastor with better boundaries. It's not a pastor's place to police my faith either."

"You young people and your 'boundaries'." When he puts "boundaries" in air quotes, I almost laugh. "It's been over six months now, and you haven't found a new church. I wonder why that is, Livvy?"

"Dad, she's taking her time," Vanessa says. "She's tried churches, but she wants to find one that feels like home."

He huffs, shaking his head. "She only tries these woke churches. Churches that tell her she can do whatever she wants. You're just looking for a way to sin and tell yourself that you aren't. But you know." His voice grows hushed. "You know what you're doing."

Goodness, he's so melodramatic. "Dad, I'm not going to do this with you. I don't need you to agree with me, but if you can't even make an effort to understand where I'm coming from, we won't be having these discussions. We're done here."

He shakes his head. "This isn't the Livvy I know."

His expression is grim and disappointed, and I hate that it makes my eyes prickle. I hate that I want to reach out and hug him and beg him to forgive me for betraying him.

"If you're going to be living a life of a sin," he says, "you need to start looking for your own place. I can't have this in my home."

I grit my teeth, willing the tears away. It's not like it means anything. He's not going to kick me out. My dad is all bluster and drama. The last time he made this threat was when he found out I watched an episode of *Euphoria* in our living room. He said, "That show is pornography, and pornography invites demons into the household." It was almost laughable, but I still sobbed and begged for his forgiveness.

I guess I have made progress, even if my instinct to submit is still there.

As soon as walks out of the kitchen, I let the tears fall.

Vanessa wraps her arms around me. "He's so fucking dramatic."

I can't help but giggle even as more tears fall. I love that she swears sometimes. I still have a hard time swearing. Maybe her future is more hopeful than mine.

"I know."

"'Living a life of sin,'" she quotes, mimicking my dad's deep and slow cadence. "I hate it when he uses his pastor voice to call us out on things. It's so manipulative." She squeezes me tightly. "And he doesn't really mean it. He doesn't even like it when you drive at night. He would never kick you out."

"I know."

"Don't cry." Her tone is pleading.

"I'm okay, love. It's just hard."

"I know. I promise I won't be an asshole anymore."

"You're not an asshole." I wipe under my eyes with the pads of my fingers, "just a little bratty sometimes."

When my phone buzzes, my gaze darts to the counter, and Cole's name flashes on the screen. My stomach both sinks and flutters at the same time. When I swipe the screen, my breath catches.

Cole: I know I said we should take time to think, but I need to see you. I did a lot of thinking during

the night, and I have an answer for you. Let's go on a hike and talk.

"What?" Vanessa asks, and the sharpness in her tone tells me my shock must be all over my face.

Warmth washes through me, sending tingles everywhere. "I think Cole is going to say yes."

TWELVE

Cole

MY HEART STARTS to pound when I catch sight of Livvy's gray Camry in my rearview mirror. I take a deep breath as she parallel parks a few cars behind me. She hops out of the car, and her curvy form in those tight workout clothes makes my stomach clench.

I'll have my hands all over that body in a few hours.

I had every intention of saying no to her two days ago. I had every intention of putting our friendship above my own desires.

Sometimes defeat is blissful.

When she gets close to my car, I step outside. She smiles at me—a sweet smile that makes something twinge in my chest, but somehow, I can't stop my gaze from grazing down her body. My God, those thick thighs and hips... That soft belly and those huge tits nearly bursting out of her shirt. She has the body of a goddess.

I can't believe I'll actually be able to touch her.

"Are you okay?" she asks, her brow furrowing.

"Yeah, I'm fine."

"What's going on? I can tell just by looking at you that you have a lot on your mind."

God, how does she do that? How does she always know when I'm upset? I wasn't even thinking about the incident with my dad, but somehow, she always knows.

"It's a long story, but basically, my parents are finally getting a divorce."

"Oh, Cole," she says, just like I knew she would. Just like I craved. "Do you want a hug, or do you need space?"

Space. As if I would ever really want that from her, even when I'd specifically asked for it.

I smile faintly. "A hug would be nice."

She doesn't waste a moment. Her footsteps patter over the gravel, and she wraps her arms around me and presses her soft body against mine. If she knew the direction of my thoughts, or how many times I've accepted her affection while fantasizing about pinning her against a wall and sinking into her warmth, she'd be terrified.

Or maybe she wouldn't be. She surprised me last night.

"I'm so sorry." Her words are muffled against my chest. "That's so awful."

"No, it's not. It's been a long time coming. I'm not going to let a divorce devastate me."

"We usually don't have a choice about what devastates us."

My throat constricts. "Yeah, but I don't want to be selfish. Having to start a new life is going to be so hard on my mom. I need to be there for her."

"Cole." Her voice is both gentle and scolding. "Your pain has nothing to do with your mom's. If you want to be able to take care of her, you need to take care of yourself first."

My fingers brush down her back. "You're an angel."

"Don't call me an angel for saying what anyone who cares for you should say." She burrows her head into my chest, and I relish it. God, touching her feels so good. Two days ago, I would have pushed her away by now, afraid that her proximity would make me feel things I shouldn't. I can't believe I've been missing this all these years.

I squeeze her once more before pulling away. There's no need to indulge her touch too much.

There's plenty of time for that.

I pull out the small plastic bag in my pocket. "I brought these for you. They're weed truffles."

Her brow knits as her gaze drops to the package. "I don't know if right now is a good time for me to try weed. Not when you need me."

I shake my head sharply. "Just being with you is enough."

As she stares down at the package, her eyes widen. She looks as intrigued as a naughty little kid.

God, she's so cute.

"I can't believe it's weed. They look like real truffles."

I smile. "They're good truffles, too. Not only are they delicious, but two of them barely made me high, which means one will be perfect for you."

She bites her lip, looking lost in thought. It's as if she's trying to decide how naughty she wants to be. "Alright, hand one over."

I pull out a truffle and set it in her hand. She smiles and pops it into her mouth, her eyes growing lazy as she chews.

Oh God, I've always loved watching her eat chocolate. How did I ever think I would be able to resist having sex with her when I've always been such a filthy bastard?

We start walking in the direction of the trail, and I lag a little behind so I can watch the adorable, bouncy sway of her hips and the slight jiggle of her ass in the tight yoga pants.

"So how are you doing?" she asks, peeking over her shoulder to glance back at me.

Thankful for the distraction from my horny thoughts, I catch up to her. "Really not that bad. I knew it was coming."

"You sound like you're trying to convince yourself more than me."

When the trail widens, I step beside her. The afternoon sun is just above the hills, right in our line of sight. I reach into my pocket and pull out my sunglasses. "Probably. I don't know... I always thought I wanted my dad to suffer for being such a colossally shitty husband, but now that he really is suffering..."

Livvy nods slowly, but she keeps her eyes fixed on the trail ahead. Her breathlessness draws my gaze to her chest, which is already rising and falling rapidly. I smile as I slow my pace. Every time I take her here, I walk too fast, forgetting how much smaller she is than me.

I'll have to remember that tonight, so I don't crush her.

God, I can't believe this is all actually going to happen.

"Can we save this conversation for after the weed kicks in?" I ask. "Actually, would you mind if we just talked about you? You're always my favorite distraction."

A shy smile touches her lips. "Sure. What do you want to talk about?"

"How has it been with your family lately? Your parents are strict as hell. Do they have any idea about the changes you're going through with your religion?"

"They know a little, but I'm not going to tell them everything. That's what the old Livvy would do. Now I know they aren't entitled to any part of my life I'm not comfortable sharing."

"You're better than I would be. I wouldn't tell them a damn thing if they were my parents."

"Yeah. The problem is they try to use religion to control me, and they need to know it won't work anymore. I actually just had to deal with it all this morning." She rolls her eyes. "My dad says I'm living in sin."

I grit my teeth, biting back my initial retort. *Your dad is a prick, and I've been wanting to call him one to his face from the moment I met him.* "I can't imagine what that must be like."

She huffs, shaking her head. "He even threatened to kick me out."

My mouth drops open, and a raging heat washes over my skin. "That's fucking ridiculous. You haven't done anything wrong."

"I know." She sighs. "But it's okay, because he won't really do it."

"Well, if he does, you know where you're living."

A sad smile tugs at her lips. "You don't have room for me in your guesthouse."

I would if you shared my bed.

Fuck, these thoughts are coming unbidden now that I'm so close to having her.

"I'm not staying in it much longer. I'll be starting at Walker Industries next week, and my parents offered to give me an advance on my inheritance if I want to buy a house. I wasn't planning on doing it since I'll be making enough money soon enough, but if you need a place to live, I'll just say fuck it and take the money."

When she sucks in her lips to repress a smile, my cheeks warm. "I know, I know. I hear myself say these things sometimes, and even I'm like, 'shut the fuck up, you rich prick.'"

"No. It's amazing that you can buy a house."

"If you need to live with me, I'll take a big advance and get something you love. A house in West Beach with a view of the ocean."

I reach out and grab her hand. She looks startled at first, but then she interlocks her fingers with mine. I never used to allow myself even this type of touch—the softer, more affectionate kind.

Letting go is heaven.

Out of the corner of my eye, I see her shake her head. "It won't come to that. He's not really going to kick me out. This is what he does. He's very dramatic. Everything he said this morning is exactly what I expected, so even though it's taxing, at least I was prepared. It's Vanessa I'm worried about. I think she feels like I'm betraying her."

"Damn." I frown. "She's always seemed like she's a lot more —" My lips close just in time. Good God, was I really about to say I thought her younger sister was more level-headed in her beliefs? How fucking condescending.

"Cole, it's okay." Livvy's voice is full of understanding. "You were going to say that Vanessa isn't as kooky of a Christian as I was at her age."

I halt in my tracks and pull her around to face me. There's a sheepish smile planted on her face.

"I was *not* going to say that. I've never thought you were kooky."

Her smile grows a little exasperated. "Cole."

"I *didn't*. Ever. Even though I didn't understand your beliefs, I've always thought you're one of the best people I know. I thought Christians were full of shit until I met you, and I'll be honest, I still think a lot of them are. But not you."

Her smile fades. "I didn't mean to upset you, but I *was* kooky. Even I can see that now. And come on, you have to admit you thought so too. At least a little bit."

I shake my head sharply. "I thought some of your beliefs were strange. And wrong, if I'm being honest. I mean, all the stuff you're trying to get rid of. The purity culture stuff. I thought it was a little weird."

"It's really weird."

"But I never thought *you* were. You marveled me when I first met you. I couldn't believe someone could be so kind and thoughtful without any strings attached." I shake my head slowly, memories flooding through me in rush. She was the first person to ask me if something was wrong five years ago. I was able to talk to her about it because she never made me feel stupid. I thought it was ridiculous that I couldn't just get over my dad's infidelity, but she didn't. That closeness with her made me realize what was really wrong.

I was lonely. I lost two people that day. My relationship with my dad was over, and my relationship with my mom was never the same. I couldn't burden her with the petty concerns of my life anymore. Not when she was so miserable.

In a strange way, I'm glad it all happened that way, because I never would have transferred to San Marcos if I hadn't been so depressed, and then I would have missed out on the most precious relationship in my life.

"Yeah, well..." she says, pulling me out of my head. "Most of who I am comes from my obedience. I was taught to be kind and thoughtful, and I always do as I'm told."

"Whatever it was, it caught my seventeen-year-old heart." I smile. "God, I would have done anything for you back then. I even thought about becoming a Christian."

Livvy halts in place. When she turns to face me, her eyes are wide and dazed. "Did you really?"

Fuck, why did I bring that up? I can't ever tell her about the church thing. How can I explain it? *I went, and I didn't like it. I was so bored I wrote college essays in my head so that the precious two hours of my weekend wouldn't be wasted.* Even now that she's more understanding about everything, she couldn't help but feel a division between us.

"I mean...sort of. Before I really understood what it meant to you. Before I knew it was a whole way of life and not just something I could attend once a week. I think I was mostly just thinking about getting laid. I was too dumb and horny to recognize the irony of that."

She doesn't return my smile. She doesn't even move.

I frown. "Does that weird you out?"

"No, I'm just...surprised." Her throat works. "Do you mean you wanted to date me back then?"

I try to gauge her reaction. She had to know I had a crush on her back then. "Of course. It wasn't obvious? I mean, remember when we had our *Lord of the Rings* marathon, and I made it a whole themed night? I played the soundtrack, and didn't I make some kind of *Lord of the Rings* inspired stew for you?"

She purses a smile. "You did."

"I don't even like The *Lord of the Rings* that much. I had to ask Zac all kinds of questions so that you wouldn't know I had never read any of the books. He made fun of me for weeks after that. I wouldn't have done it if I wasn't..."

My lips close. Holy fuck, was I about to say "in love"? Being so close to having her is making me crazy.

"Really into you," I finish.

She stares at me for what feels like an eternity, and I strain to read the look in her eyes.

"What changed?" she finally asks in a small voice.

She stares at me steadily, without even a flicker of understanding in her eyes, and I guess I shouldn't be surprised. The day she told me she could never be with an atheist was probably just an ordinary moment for her. It isn't burned into her memory like it is mine. She didn't mean it as a personal rejection.

But goddamn, it sure felt like one.

"You told me you could only be with a Christian who was as 'on fire for God' as you were. I didn't really know what that meant, but I knew it wasn't me."

She nods slowly. "I was so extreme. Was that what made your crush go away?"

"What do you mean?"

"I mean, if you really liked me at first—*like* liked me—and now you can only see me as a friend. Did my faith make your crush go away?"

I stare at her for a moment. "No... I guess... It never went anywhere. You just became much more to me than a crush."

LIVVY

IT NEVER WENT ANYWHERE.

The words echo as an audible voice as we sit on our favorite boulder at the top of the peak. The Santa Barbara coast stretches out below us, and the ocean is electric under the afternoon sky. I've lived in this city my entire life, and yet it's like I'm seeing it for the first time.

Why did I take that edible? Now I'm forced to mull over his confession in a brain fog. Every time I try to hang on to a thought, it slips out of my grasp. But my body remembers. My stomach is still fluttering, and heat shoots into my groin every time the words replay in my head.

You became much more to me than a crush.

How is it possible that my deepest, most secret fantasy—

that he's in love with me and doesn't know it—might really be coming true?

Goodness, am I dreaming?

I lift my foot into the air. My shoe looks just like I remember. That tiny brown stain on the toe is still there from when I spilled my Hazelnut Mocha almost a year ago. This image is too specifically accurate. In a dream, my shoes would change color, or look strange somehow.

Cole's laughter only strengthens my certainty. This heat creeping up my neck and seeping into my cheeks is more tingly and electric than normal, but it's certainly real. It's embarrassment, though it feels like it's coming from far away. He's laughing at *me*. Because I'm staring at my shoe.

Goodness, I'm as high as the seagulls flying over us. Their squawks send a shiver down my spine. "I don't like seagulls," I say in a rush.

"No?" I hear a smile in his voice.

I shake my head, trying to think of a way to save myself from my blunder. "They're mean. Cruel, even. I've seen them beat up on other birds."

"Maybe that's what they have to do to survive." When I still hear that smile, I know my save wasn't as calm and measured as it sounded in my head. Why am even talking about seagulls?

"Survival never justifies cruelty," I say.

"I don't think seagulls reflect much on morality, but I guess I shouldn't speak for them."

I open my mouth and close it. What was I going to say about morals? It was there just a moment ago, rising to my tongue, and now it's gone.

His deep chuckle makes heat wash over my skin. When I whip around, he's looking at me with an almost pained expression. "I'm sorry." He sucks in his lips, but his chest still shakes.

"You're just so cute. You should see your face. If I were a dick, I would take a video."

A warm smile rises to my mouth. He's so sweet for bringing the edible today and helping me work through my contract when he's clearly going through his own stuff.

"I shouldn't even be high," I say. "Not when you're sad."

He reaches out and picks at a weed poking out from a crevice in the rock. "I'm not sad."

"Of course you are."

"No." His gaze stays fixed on the little leaf between his fingers. "I want him to get what he deserves for destroying my mom's life."

My gaze shifts to the bright blue sky, and my murky thoughts grow sharp and focused. I see Cole's mom, calm and a little demure, but not destroyed. "Did she tell you that?"

"What?"

"That he destroyed her life?"

"God, no. She doesn't do that. She would never burden me with their marital problems. She didn't even want me to tell her what happened in Arizona."

Ah, Arizona. The trip he went on with his dad a few months before I met him. He's only ever told me about it in scattered pieces.

"What happened exactly?" I keep my voice very soft. "I feel like you censored a lot of it when you first told me."

He laughs humorlessly, and it's a brittle sound that makes me want to hug him. "I caught him in the act. I actually saw him fucking another woman. It was..." he shivers, "...disgusting."

He jumps a little when I set my hand on his arm. "And probably traumatic," I say.

"I don't know. I hardly remember it."

Because you were traumatized, and that's how some people

cope. Thank God, I'm not so high that I let that slip out. He's trying be tough about this, and I'll let him put on the show, since he's probably doing it mostly for himself. If he were ready to share his true feelings, he would have done it with me already.

I lift my hand and run my fingers up his arm and onto his shoulder, surprised at my boldness. I don't think it's the weed chocolate. It's something else. Something shifted between us today.

It feels like a new beginning.

"I would have been traumatized if I were you. My dad was my hero when I was seventeen. It would have broken my heart to see him doing something like that."

"You're an angel." He grabs my hand and squeezes it before interlocking his fingers with mine. He lifts it to his lips and presses a soft kiss against my skin. "But I think it was good that I found out the way I did. I became much more realistic about love and relationships after that."

"What do you mean?"

"I don't think romantic love is real. It's all based on attraction, and that fades over time."

I frown. "You think that just because it faded for your dad?"

"I think it fades for everyone, and they all pretend like it doesn't."

A tingling ripple runs over my skin. I always thought his whole "I-don't-do-relationships" thing—which Mari claims only the worst fuck-boys say—was just a symptom of his youth. I thought for sure he would start to feel differently once he got out of college and was ready to settle here in Santa Barbara.

What does this mean for us?

His tender smile pulls me out of my reverie. "Is your brain getting a little fuzzy again?"

I shake my head. "I was thinking about all the couples I know who've stayed married until death."

"Yeah, but that doesn't mean they were in love. Or happy."

"It depends on..." My lips close. What was I about to say?

He grins as he brushes a strand of hair behind my ears. "Don't think too hard, Angel."

When I glare at him, his smile grows.

"I'm not that high anymore," I say.

"No, of course not."

"I actually feel myself thinking more deeply than I usually do."

"Naturally."

When I narrow my eyes, he chuckles.

"Love goes through phases," I say, thankful I seem to have regained my voice. "Sometimes it's passionate, and sometimes it's more like friendship, but that doesn't mean it isn't there."

He stares at me for a long moment. "Maybe for some really lucky people, but I don't think that's generally the case. Monogamy just isn't realistic. I don't even think humans were meant for it."

I sigh heavily. I can't handle an anthropological argument about love and monogamy right now. "You can't have real love without risk."

He squeezes my hand tightly. His dark-brown eyes bore into mine, sparkling in the afternoon sunlight. "I disagree with that completely. It's not real love if you can't count on it. I think we can only find real love in friendship. That's why I didn't jump at the opportunity to take your virginity. Bringing sex into our friendship might complicate something that's perfect as it is."

My throat grows too tight to speak. Jesus, please say he isn't about to reject me.

"But I'm going to do it anyway."

A heaviness pulls at my body, making my eyelids fall shut.

"It's important to you, and I want to help you," he says, "because you've given me so much over the years. More than you could ever know."

My eyes pop open. "I don't want you doing it out of obligation."

He laughs softly, lifting his hand and brushing his fingers along my cheek. "An obligation." His voice is husky as he leans forward and presses his warm lips against mine. "What a chore it's going to be." He sets his hand on my thigh and starts trailing it upward. "Torture. Absolute torture."

He withdraws from me suddenly, grabs my shoulders, and pins me with a hard stare. "I want you to be mine for all of this week."

My head begins to swim. "The whole week?"

"I start work next Monday, and I'm going to be busy as hell after that. I want to do this right. There's no need to rush into having sex when you haven't tried anything else, and I definitely don't want to rush..." He brushes his lips against mine before pulling away. "I want your whole week. Every moment of it. I probably won't even let you out of my bed. Can you do that for me?"

I nod slowly, feeling hypnotized.

His jaw hardens. "I might scare you. I didn't save my virginity for you, so this won't be anything like what you imagined for your first time. I'm a heathen with lots of experience, and you're going to find out what I've wanted to do to you all these years. Do you think you can handle it?"

Fire courses through my belly. "I think I'll like it."

"We'll see." His expression grows fierce. "You're mine for the next week. Cancel any plans you have. Tell your parents you're staying with Mari or something, because you won't be seeing them at all. We leave my bed to eat, and that's it."

I release a nervous giggle. "I can't believe this is happening."

I really can't. This is what I've always wanted from him—for him to be as greedy for my touch as he is for my time and attention. It feels like a dream, but even in my dreamy state of mind, I'm certain it's real.

A real possibility for our future.

If this week is as spectacular as I think it could be, he might decide our friendship isn't "perfect as it is". He'll see it could be so much more. We have all the ingredients for the strongest kind of relationship, the kind he doesn't believe in now.

We have passion as well as friendship. Maybe passion fades, like he fears. Or maybe it ebbs and flows, like I've always thought. Either way, we have friendship to sustain us. We wouldn't end up like his parents.

I just hope I can help him see that.

THIRTEEN

Livvy

"OKAY," Mari says, "so the story is that we're staying with Brenna for the week, and I'll actually stay with her so that my parents can corroborate if my dad mentions anything the next time he and your dad hang out."

"Ugh!" I groan as I rummage through my underwear drawer. "I have only granny panties."

Coming down from that stupid edible has frayed my nerves, and having to pack for a whole week with Cole has made me both giddy and sick to my stomach.

"I hate that I'm lying like a little kid," I say. "I need to just tell my parents everything and get it over with. It's so stupid that you have to change all of your plans for the week just so I can get laid. I'm a grown woman. I need to act like one."

"You don't need that kind of pressure right now. Just enjoy your week and think about all of that after. It's no problem for me at all. It gives me a chance to get out of the house for a bit."

After sifting through the drawer once more, I slam it shut. I turn around, march to my bed, and plop myself down next to Mari, my eyes prickling. "I don't have anything sexy."

She sets her hands on my shoulders and kneads her thumbs against the tight muscles at the base of my neck. "He won't care what your underwear looks like. Once you get started, he's going to get you naked as fast as he can."

Normally, hearing something like that would warm my insides, but my gut is churning with a coldness that won't go away. What if it's terrible? What if *I'm* terrible, and I can see it in his eyes right after we have sex?

"Fuck abstinence only education," I raise my voice, unable to help myself.

Mari's eyes grow huge. "Wow. I think that's maybe the second time ever that I've heard you say fuck."

"I didn't even go to sex ed. Did I ever tell you that?"

Her expression softens. "Yeah, I think so."

I laugh humorlessly. "My parents signed a waiver. I went to the office and did homework during sex ed. I thought I'd learn more about sex in my college classes, but it turns out, they don't go into much detail about the mechanics, because you're supposed to already know. Everything I've learned about sex came from purity conferences. The only penis I've ever seen was a cartoon, and it had a big green cartoon STD on it. It looked like a monster."

Mari sucks in her lips, as if she's fighting laugher. I can't help but smile, even as my insides roil. "It's sad," I say.

"It is sad, but it's not your fault."

"It doesn't matter." My voice is brittle. "It doesn't change the fact that I have no idea what to do when it comes to sex."

"It doesn't take that long to learn, and if you're nervous because you think Cole's not going to enjoy having sex with you, you're out of your mind. You could just lie there, and he'd be happy."

"That's just not true, and you know it. I've heard you talk about people who were bad at sex."

Her brows draw together. "That's different. I didn't have years of emotional investment. I've never been in love with anyone I've had sex with, and given everything he said today, I'm pretty sure he's in love with you."

I groan. "Our relationship hasn't been tested, and I hate myself for feeling this way. My impurity contract was all about me and my journey at first, and now I'm letting it become about Cole. Just like I always do."

"Then take ownership now. Prioritize your needs. It's not all about pleasing Cole. He needs to please you."

"And I'm sure he will, because he knows how, but I've never learned anything." I shake my head. "I wish I had watched porn."

"Why don't we watch some right now?" She pulls out her phone and swipes her thumb over the screen. "I really only watch lesbian porn, because straight porn is way too male gaze-y, but I'm sure I can find something decent..."

I shut my eyes, laughing softly. "No, wait. Don't do that. I can't learn everything in two hours, and it'll probably only make me more nervous."

"Tell Cole that. Tell him you're nervous and don't know what to do. I know he'll be understanding."

"Of course he will, but I don't want him to be understanding. I want him to be wildly turned on. I want to give him the best sex he's ever had."

Because I want to convince him to be with me, but I can't say that to Mari. She would rightly tell me that I'm slipping back into my old patterns.

If I want to be in a relationship with him, I need to say

something instead of passively waiting for him wake up and realize he's madly in love with me.

This week can't just be about sex. If I really want to assert myself and start asking for the things I want, I have to also make myself vulnerable. I told him today that you can't have love without risk, and I am only now recognizing my hypocrisy. Of the two of us, I'm the biggest coward.

FOURTEEN

Cole

SHE'S HERE.

She parked her car outside my house a moment ago, and her little footsteps are right now sounding along the concrete. I rush over to the front door and open it before she even gets the chance to knock. The sight of her standing at the threshold sends a wave of possessiveness over me. She's wearing a T-shirt and sweats—probably because she knows there's no point in dressing up since we'll be naked most of the time—and a duffel bag hangs from her shoulder.

She's here to stay.

She's mine.

I pull her into my arms and kiss the soft skin on her neck. I keep my hand on her lower back as I guide her inside.

"You're so much touchier than you usually are with me," she says.

I smile and lead her into the kitchen. "I'm going to get a lot touchier than this."

She glances at the platter of baked ziti on the table and smiles. "You made dinner."

"I tried. You know I'm not the best cook, so don't get your hopes up." I grab the bag from her shoulder. "How about I unpack this while you start eating?"

Her brow knits. "It's not that much stuff. I don't really see the need to unpack."

I shake my head. "You're unpacking. I cleared a drawer in my bathroom and made space in my closet. For the next week, you live here."

When a childish grin spreads over her face, something twinges in my chest. She's just as excited at the thought of her living here as I am.

"This feels so naughty," she says.

My brow furrows, even as a smile tugs at lips. "Unpacking your bag is the least naughty thing you'll be doing this week."

"You don't understand. Living with your boyfriend is one of the worst things a Christian girl can do. Having sex with your boyfriend is one thing, because even if you do it multiple times, you can always tell yourself you just messed up, but living with him is committing yourself to a life of sin..." Her smile fades.

"What?"

"I just called you my boyfriend."

I ought to be alarmed that I didn't even notice, but it seems like nothing can drown out the euphoria of finally letting go. I shoot her a reassuring smile and lean forward to kiss her on the cheek. "It's okay. I basically am your boyfriend for the week. Alright, eat up. I'll join you in a minute."

After walking into my bedroom, I set her bag on my bed and

unzip it. A pair of pink pajama shorts sits right at the top, and something about the sight of it makes my stomach flip over. I've never seen her wear pajamas before. During the countless hours we've spent together, there have always been strict boundaries.

As much as I want her naked this whole week, a part of me craves to see her as she is on a regular night, wearing these little shorts. I want to watch her brush her teeth with her hair damp from the shower. I want to wait quietly on my bed while she writes in her prayer journal, as I know she does every night.

I want every part of her that I've missed.

"Oh my gosh, the ziti is delicious," she calls out, and I smile to myself.

It's not delicious. I tried a bite of it already, but she's always overly enthusiastic about the food I make for her. Maybe even especially when it isn't particularly good, as if she's worried I'll pick up on the fact that she doesn't like it and my feelings will be hurt. It's one of her many small kindnesses that made me fall like a ton of bricks in those first few months we were becoming friends.

"I left it in the oven too long," I call back. "The cheese got brown."

"No, I love burnt cheese!"

"Eat up, then. I don't want you to be hungry tonight, not with what I have planned for you."

"Okay." Her voice is much fainter this time. Is that nervousness?

I grab one of her dresses and put it on a hanger. After setting it in the closet next to one of my shirts, a tingling sensation runs over my skin.

How am I ever going to let her leave here? How am I going to share a bed with her for a week and then let her walk out of here forever, taking this little dress out of my closet as she returns to her old life, to our regular friendship?

I'll think about this later.

After I finish unpacking her things, I join her in the kitchen. When my gaze falls to her plate, I want to smile yet again. She's barely even nibbled at her ziti, despite her supposed love of burnt cheese. "Livvy, if it's inedible, you won't hurt my feelings. We can find something on Grubhub."

"No, it's not that." The shake of her head is jerky, and my gaze falls to her lap where her hands are pressed firmly together. Warmth washes over me when understanding dawns. I sit next to her and grab her hand. As expected, it's stiff and damp. "You're nervous."

"Yeah."

"What can I do?"

She scrapes at her top lip with her bottom teeth. "Can we talk a little bit? About what we're going to do?"

Even as anxious as I am, my dick can't help but stir at her words. It's going to be difficult to talk about it without wanting to throw her over my shoulder and carry her into my bedroom, but I can do it. "Of course," I rasp.

Her gaze falls to her lap. "I'm about to be really open and vulnerable right now, and you're probably going to laugh, but I just need to say it."

Tenderness squeezes my chest tightly. I scoot my chair closer to her, set my hand on her back, and run my fingers up and down the soft skin at the base of her neck. "I'm not going to laugh. I promise."

"I have no idea what to do with a penis."

I clench my jaw tightly, engaging all of my facial muscles to keep my expression blank. I hold my breath to keep the hovering laughter from bursting out. Oh God, that took me by surprise. I swallow and nod slowly.

"And I know you have low expectations because you know I have no experience. And you'll be understanding if I don't touch it right or move right or whatever, but the thing is, I'm very scared of things that are unfamiliar to me. I know this sounds really silly, but basically...I'm scared of your penis."

My face is straining to keep my lips from twitching. I want to reassure her, but I'm afraid my voice might crack. I twirl my finger around a strand of hair at the back of her head. "That's okay." I speak very softly.

"Cole." Her tone is scolding, though her lips quirk. "Just laugh, okay? I know you're trying not to."

"No, I'm not," I say, but my lips are twitching now.

She rolls her eyes. "The fact that you're not laughing is even more annoying."

When my chest starts to vibrate, I avert my face from hers and cover my mouth. She hits me gently on the shoulder. "I hate you. You should have just laughed from the beginning."

"I'm sorry." My throat is tight. "I totally get what you were trying to say. It was just...the way you said it. 'I'm scared of your penis'."

"It's the pathetic truth."

My laughter fades. "It's not pathetic. I'm glad you told me."

"I had to tell you. I had to get it out of the way now, because I know in the heat of the moment, I'll be too ashamed to admit it. I was hoping we could agree now that you'll tell me exactly what I need to do. Like, spell it out to me. Maybe even show me. It might be unsexy, but it will make me so much less anxious."

I reach out and grab her by the waist, and her eyes widen as I lift her up and set her in my lap. She smiles as she lifts her knees and snuggles against my chest. God, she's so soft.

"I don't want you to be anxious." I brush my lips along her head. "And it's not unsexy. I probably would have gotten better a lot sooner at making women come if I had just outright asked how they wanted me to touch them."

"Did you used to be bad at sex?" Her voice is full of disbelief.

I lift a hand and tuck a strand of hair behind her ear. "I don't think anyone is good at sex when they first start out. It takes a while to learn what you like, and how to give other people what they like."

"That's part of why I'm nervous. You have years more experience."

I squeeze her tightly. "You don't have to be nervous. I'm going to enjoy whatever we do, but I'm relieved you're comfortable enough to tell me what you're feeling."

She nods. "I think sexual communication is really important. I'm glad that you do too."

My throat constricts as I kiss her on the cheek.

Oh God, I've never loved anything more than I love her.

"How about we do this," I say. "We won't even worry about my penis. We'll pretend it's not even there. I'll keep my scary penis in my pants, and tonight will just be about you."

Her face falls. "I want you to enjoy yourself."

I snort. "I'll definitely enjoy myself."

"But not fully."

"Livvy, trust me. I will *fully* enjoy myself."

"But you'll be sexually frustrated when we're done."

I shake my head. "I'll jack off in the shower later. When I first met you, I used to do it after almost every time we hung out."

Her eyes grow huge. "Did you really?"

I grin darkly as I squeeze the skin around her waist. "I told you I'm a filthy bastard."

She frowns. "Then I must be too, because I think about you almost every time I masturbate."

"What?"

When her eyes widen, I realize I nearly shouted at her. She

swallows and averts her gaze from mine. "Yeah... I mean, sometimes I think about hot celebrities, but it's usually you."

I make my body grow very still, not wanting to spook her. "What do you think about?"

She smiles shyly. "That I could never tell anyone. Maybe Mari... But I don't think I could share the details even with her. Trust me when I tell you that Christian girl fantasies are twisted, and it's not just me. Purity culture messes with our heads. Mari thinks I should do my master's thesis about it if I end up going to grad school."

"Twisted how?"

She smiles, and her cheeks grow pink. "Cole, trust me. It's weird. Like, I would be totally fine telling you if I thought it would turn you on, but I'm positive it won't."

I grip her at the back of her neck and force her to look at me. "Let me be the judge of that. Tell me, Angel."

LIVVY

ANGEL.

I love it when he says it like that, like it's a filthy word instead of an endearment I don't deserve.

His fingers cut into my neck as I stare up at his face. Those blazing dark eyes are fixed on my face, and his jaw is hard. He looks like he wants to spank me, and goodness, I think I'd like it if he did.

"It's too embarrassing," I say.

He grips my neck tighter, and it sends an electric heat into my belly.

"You can do it." His jaw ticks. "Shut your eyes. Pretend I'm not here."

Something about the commanding tone of his voice makes my eyes fall shut of their own will. "I think about being hunted. We're in a forest, and you're chasing me."

"Why am I chasing you?"

"Because you want to..." My lips close. Why can't I get the words out when I think he'll like them?

I gasp when he yanks my head back and presses a kiss against my neck. "You can say it. Tell me why I'm chasing you."

"You want to fuck me."

He groans against my neck. "Good girl." He slides his hand along my thigh and up under my shirt before settling on my belly. The warmth of his skin sends a tingle into my groin. "Tell me more."

Oh my God, I can't believe this is happening. I can't believe he's talking to me like this.

"In my fantasy," I say, "you're a stranger, but it's you. Do you know what I mean?"

"Yes." His voice is rough.

"I'm running for my life, because I'm not really sure what you're going to do to me."

"What are you afraid I'm going to do?"

"I don't know."

He squeezes my neck, and I let out a gasp. "Yes, you do. Be a good girl and tell me."

I swallow. "I'm not sure if you're going to fuck me or hurt me, and for some reason, knowing it could be either one really turns me on."

He groans, and the sound drifts over my body like warm water. Goodness, he really likes this, and here I thought I was a deviant for even thinking it.

His fingers slip into my pants, and my gut clenches as they trail their way downward, stopping just at the edge of my underwear. "What do I do when I finally catch you?" he asks.

I open my mouth and shut it, wincing afterward. "This is the really embarrassing part."

"Tell me, Angel." His warm breath tickles my ear. When he slips his hand into my underwear and settles his fingers on my clit, the breath leaves my lungs in a rush. "I'll reward you."

His fingers start to move, and I'm lost. Lost like I am at night when I escape to this dark, primitive world that provides my only wild escape from my pristine life.

"You pin me down by the arms and press your hips against mine," I say, "so I can't move. You tell me I can try to get away, but you won't let me. And then you shove yourself inside me."

"Oh fuck, Livvy." His voice is a rasp. When he starts rubbing me lighter and more quickly, I whimper. "Is this really what you think about?"

Hot shame washes over me suddenly. When I try to pull away, he squeezes my neck firmly. "I didn't mean that as a judgment. It makes me crazy to know you think about these things. Can you feel me right now?" When he moves his hips forward, something hard and sharp presses against my butt. "If I had known this years ago, I would have devoured you."

"You don't think it's kind of a deviant fantasy?"

He presses a hard kiss against my cheek. "No, I really don't. You're not hurting anyone. It's just for you. And now that you've shared it with me, it's making me lose my mind. Tell me more."

The lull of his voice is both comforting and erotic at once. It took me years to realize there's something deeply titillating about being forced to do the thing I desperately wanted but was always forbidden.

I lean my back into his shoulder. "You cover my mouth to make sure I don't make a sound."

His groan is almost pained. "Because you'd be loud. I know you'd be loud." His lips graze my cheek, and the pace of his fingers grows more rapid, making my stomach grow taut.

"I don't know if I'd be loud. I'm not loud when I touch myself. I only make a sound when I..."

When he halts the movement of his fingers, I hunch forward.

"Say it," he commands. "Say it."

Oh God, I love this. I love having him order me to do the things that have always made me scared and ashamed. I thrust my hips to get more of the touch I crave.

"No." He withdraws his fingers further. "Not until you say it."

I take a small breath. "When I come."

He kisses my shoulder. "Good girl."

When he returns his fingers to my clit, the up-and-down motion is much more frantic. "I really like it when you talk like that," I say breathlessly.

"When I call you a good girl?"

"Yeah."

"You are a good girl. Such a good girl to tell me your fantasy and use filthy words. Do you want me to reward you? Do you want me to make you come?"

"Yeah... Please."

"Oh fuck, Livvy. I've always wanted to hear you say that."

He removes his fingers from my clit. I shriek when he grabs me by the waist and lifts me into the air. Chair legs scrape against the tile floor just before my back is set on the hard kitchen table.

His eyes are bright, and his jaw is set as he stares down at my hips. As he yanks down my yoga pants roughly, he looks so much like the primitive stranger Cole of my fantasy.

After tossing my pants on the floor, he grips my thighs and spreads them apart. My initial instinct is to shut them, but thankfully, his grip is too firm. His eyes are half shut as he stares between my legs. "Fuck, you're gorgeous."

Heat washes over me, pooling in my belly. My fantasies were never this specific. I never imagined him finding that part of me beautiful.

It makes me feel like a goddess.

He drops his head between my legs, nuzzles and inhales, and the heat of his breath makes me gasp. "Mmm," he hums. "I'm going to be spending a lot of time here this week."

The first brush of his tongue is like fire. Oh Jesus, that slippery softness is so much better than a finger. After only a few strokes, that familiar wave of pleasure is already building. The delicious torture makes my hips buck, but he holds them tightly.

"You taste like heaven."

His words send liquid heat into my belly. As he sucks and licks my clit, I'm pulled into the dark forest. He's caught me, and now he's feasting before he ravages me. His mouth drifts lower to...

Oh my goodness! The whimper pulled from my chest is involuntary. Where is the shame? I never imagined being licked and sucked there, and nothing but this heavenly feeling could keep me on this table.

My hips start to flail, but he holds me tightly against the table. "You can't get away," he whispers against my clit. "You're mine now."

Euphoria crashes over me, and I scream. "Oh my God!" I whimper. "Oh my God!" When the final wave of pleasure washes over me, my hips buck one last time before my whole body grows limp.

As I melt into the table, Cole's face enters my clouded vision. "You're perfect." He presses his lips against mine and slips his tongue into my mouth. I set my hand on his shoulder as I kiss him back. His body is trembling. "You're shaking," I say.

"That I am." He stands, grabs me by the hips, and lifts me. Cradling me against his chest, he carries me to the couch and sets me down gently. "I'll be right back." He smiles.

I frown as he walks into the bathroom. A few seconds later, the shower faucet turns on, and my stomach sinks. He's going to get himself off.

I don't know what happened to me after that orgasm, but the prospect of touching his penis isn't nearly as scary, especially when the alternative is waiting out here while he reaches that blissful state without me. I push myself from the couch and march toward the bathroom. Mist seeps out through the doorway, and by the time I make it inside, he's already in the shower. His big form is murky through the wet glass, but I can make out that up-and-down motion of his hand.

My languid body comes alive again.

I peel off my shirt and unhook my bra. The misty air on my bare nipples makes cold shame twist in my stomach, but I can't let it stop me. He'll like seeing me naked. I know he will.

When I open the shower door, his head jerks up, and his eyes grow wide. "Holy shit, you're naked!" His gaze roams from my chest to my hips and back to my chest again.

A giddy smile rises to my lips. "Can I help you out?"

His mouth drops open. "Fuck, I can't believe this is actually happening. Yes, of course you can. Get in here."

I keep my gaze fixed on his upper body as I step inside. Goodness, he's so beautiful. The water flows over his bare, muscled chest, and strands of his dark hair is plastered against his face. I always loved looking at him whenever we went swimming together.

This is so much better.

I can't look at his penis just yet, because if I do, I might chicken out, but it hovers just outside of my vision. I keep my gaze fixed on his face as I kneel down on the hard tile.

His dark brows draw together. "Oh fuck."

I grin up at him before finally letting my gaze fall, and the sight in front of me makes my stomach do a little turn.

Oh fuck is right.

It's big.

It's *really* big, but didn't I expect that? I don't have anything to compare it with, but he's six-foot-five and built like a lumberjack. There's no way his penis wouldn't look big to me.

I can do this. I can fit at least the tip of it in my mouth.

I look up at him. "I thought it would be veiny and scary—and ugly, if I'm being honest—but I actually like the way it looks."

His rigid expression softens a little. "It likes the way you look too, and it was already just a couple seconds from exploding so—"

I plunge forward and wrap my mouth around the tip.

"Fucking Jesus, Livvy," he shouts.

I move in the back-and-forth motion I've seen in movies, not quite sure what to do with my tongue, but he doesn't seem to mind. His skin feels a little rubbery, but not unpleasant. And hearing his big groans makes heat fill my gut.

"Livvy, honey." His voice is strangled. "I'm going to come."

I hum, and he groans again, sounding almost in pain. "Sweetheart, I can't come in your mouth. You need to pull away."

I shake my head slightly as I speed up my pace, just the way I do with my fingers when I'm close to coming. He pulses, and a small spurt of salty liquid trickles into my mouth. I suck hard, lest I lose my nerve when the rest of it comes out.

"Fuck!" he shouts, and a burst of liquid shoots into my throat. I gag a little, but I keep my mouth in place. He digs his fingers into my hair as he hunches forward. "Oh God, you're an angel."

My stomach flutters at his words and the roaring groan that follows them. As it fades into a whimper, his grip on my hair softens into a caress.

When I pull back, a little bit of come dribbles out of my mouth. I look up at him. "I guess I couldn't swallow all of it."

He releases something between a cry and a laugh and shakes his head. "I can't believe that just happened."

I stand up and wrap my arms around him, relishing the slickness of our wet bodies pressed against each other. "It was fun, and I never thought a blow job would be fun. They always sounded gross to me."

"I never thought I'd get one from you, and I've imagined it a million times. In fact, I was imagining *exactly* that just a minute ago." He squeezes me tightly. "I don't think I'm ever letting you leave this house."

I smile against his chest. "I don't want to go anywhere."

He lifts my slippery body and pulls it against his chest, pressing a hard kiss against my cheek as he carries me out of the shower. "Let's go to bed."

After gently laying me down on the mattress, he crawls in next to me and pulls me against his warm, damp body. I twist around to look at his face. "Are we going to have sex now?"

Even after all of that, nervousness flutters in my belly, but he shakes his head. His gaze grows hooded as he brushes his hand against my cheek. "Let's lie here for a little bit first. I just want to look at you."

His expression is as tender as I've ever seen, and something tugs at my chest. I recognize that look. It's a reflection of my own heart.

I think he really is in love with me, but there's only one way to find out for sure.

I can't keep holding on to my delusional hope, no matter how much it's warmed me over the years, because in the end, it's as flimsy as an old baby blanket. It's preventing me from moving forward and growing. If he doesn't love me, if he doesn't want to be with me, I need to know.

After he takes my virginity, I'm going to tell him how I feel.

FIFTEEN

Cole

HER DEEP BREATH makes a little rumbling sound. She furrows her brow and rolls onto her stomach, mumbling softly. A smile rises to my lips. She roused herself from sleep with her own snore.

Now would be the perfect time to wake her up with a kiss, but I won't do it. I'm just going to keep watching her, like the sap I've become over the past half hour I've been awake.

She's the most beautiful thing I've ever seen, and it makes me want to weep.

Why do I feel this way? Why does seeing her lying here with her mouth open and that little furrow on her brow make my chest constrict so tightly that I can hardly take a breath, as if I'm mourning the loss of her when she's as close as she's ever been?

I'm in love with her.

I shut my eyes and roll to my back. That's what this is. The deepest love and the deepest denial. Some part of me must have known all along that if I ever got this close to her, I wouldn't be able to delude myself anymore.

Love is misery.

Even when it's as beautiful as this—with her warm body next to mine as the morning sunlight creeps into the room.

Who knows what she feels for me or how long it will last?

I'm on the path to losing her forever, and there's no getting off it now.

She stirs again, but this time, she turns onto her back, and her eyes start to creep open. When they focus on my face, a sleepy smile twinges her lips, and that ache in my chest grows sharper.

"Morning, beautiful."

"Morning?" Her voice is raspy from sleep.

"Yep." I lift my hand and tuck a strand of dark hair behind her ear. "I think that orgasm wore you out."

She blinks a few times. "I'm still a virgin."

I laugh as I press a kiss on her cheek. "I guess by your purity standards, you are. You won't be for much longer, but first, I want to take you somewhere."

"Right now?"

I smile as I glance at the window. "Yep, and we need to go soon."

A little while later, we're walking up the hill at the edge of my parents' property. It has the best view of the ocean, and even though we missed the sunrise—because it turns out my angel is a little sluggish in the morning—it's still a beautiful sight. The sun is molten, casting an orange glow over the water.

I can't believe I'm here with her. We've shared so much time together over the years, but never the morning, and there's something hauntingly intimate about seeing her with her hair still a little mussed from sleep and her nose pink from the cold air.

"Wow," Livvy says. "Do you wake up this early a lot?"

"I do not. I actually can't remember the last time I was up this early."

"This is a perfect spot for reflection. I wish I had my prayer journal—" her nose wrinkles as she stares out at the water, "—and maybe a bagel."

"We didn't have dinner last night."

She takes a step forward and peeks back over her shoulder. "No, you ate me instead."

My mouth drops open. "I think that's maybe the filthiest thing I've ever heard you say." I yank her up against me and kiss her softly on the head. "What a good girl you are."

She looks up at me, her eyes wide. "Is that always how you are? During sex, I mean?"

"Um... How?"

"Are you always so commanding?"

I smile lazily. "That's why I was afraid I'd scare you. I'm kind of...dominating during sex. I mean I don't have to be, but I knew it would be hard to hold back with you when I've been imagining it for so long." I wrap my arms around her shoulders. "I've dreamed about fucking you raw and rewarding you for taking it like a good girl."

"And I love it. Like, *really* love it. I always thought I'd be too embarrassed to enjoy sex like that, but now I don't think that at all. I think when it's like that, it makes me feel way less nervous."

My head grows heavy. I never thought she would be this way either. I thought she'd need me gentle and soft—how I usually am with her.

That fantasy. My God. *"I'm not sure if you're going to fuck me or hurt me, and for some reason, knowing it could be either one really turns me on."* I can't believe this is who she's been all these years inside that demure little exterior.

I lower my lips to hers and kiss her hard. "Come on. Let's get you fed so I can get back to commanding you."

LIVVY

AFTER DECIDING to get breakfast at a coffee shop near the wharf, we take a small trail down to the beach. The sun is high in the sky, and it brushes golden light over his face, making his brown eyes sparkle.

I'm in heaven, holding his big hand while we take a morning walk on the beach after spending the night with his arms wrapped around me. I never thought this would happen.

"I already got a text from Mariana," I say, "and she's never up this early. She wanted to know how last night went, but I feel like a text can't do it justice."

He grins. "I'm hoping I get a whole chapter in your prayer journal."

"Chapter?" I smile. "Do you think I divide my journal by chapters?"

"I've never given journaling too much thought, except for yours. I can't tell you how desperately I used to want to read it. I was tempted sometimes, especially when you brought it to school."

Heat washes over my face. "What kind of high schooler brings her prayer journal to school? Oh man, how embarrassing. No wonder I've never been laid."

He squeezes my hand as he pulls me away from the water, which is now only inches from hitting my shoes. "You won't be able to say that soon, Angel. Maybe that's what you should text Mariana. Say you'll call her after you've been good and railed."

My stomach flutters for a moment before it sinks. Cole must sense the change in my mood, because he turns to me with a questioning frown.

I swallow. "Do you know about the lie we made up for my parents about where I'm staying this week?"

"Um... Yeah, that you're staying with Mari, or going on vacation with her or something?"

"It's so elaborate and *so* stupid. The story we came up with is that we're spending the week at her friend Brenna's. We called it a weeklong slumber party. I'm not very close with Brenna, so my parents would never believe just I would go. And since my dad and Mari's dad are really good friends, Mari is actually staying with Brenna this week just to corroborate my story."

He nods slowly while licking his lips, and I can sense the direction of his thoughts. I'm a baby compared to him. He hardly even had to ask for his parents' permission back in high school. His mom even allowed him to have girls sleep over, which was unfathomable to my innocent mind back then. It must seem outrageous that I'm still letting my parents control me at twenty-one years old.

"It's ridiculous," I say. "I'm a grown woman. I know that's what you're thinking, and it's okay."

"I wasn't thinking that."

"If you weren't, you're being way too forgiving of my flaws. It's absurd, and it's just one symptom of my whole problem. I'm only still living with my parents because I was too scared to go away for college like you did."

The wind presses a dark strand of his hair against his forehead, and he brushes it away with his fingers. "It's not like I went very far. I didn't want to move too far away from you, which isn't much different than wanting to stay close to family. And you're saving money, which I didn't have to think twice about."

"Yeah, but I could have taken out loans if I really wanted the dorm experience, like Mari did her first year. Instead, I've lived basically the same life I lived in high school, even down to curfew and dating rules." I glance up at him. "Do you know that if my dad caught us holding hands right now—*just* holding hands—he would expect you to ask his permission to date me?"

His brow furrows. "Do you need me to do it? I will if it'll make things easier for you. Especially if you want to be able to go out in public this week without worrying about running into your family."

"Absolutely not. It grosses me out that he even thinks it's his permission to give. I can't believe I used to buy into all of that. When I get home at the end of the week, I plan to tell my parents I was with you."

He halts in place and pulls me around to face him, his expression probing and tender. "If you really need to tell him everything that's going on, I can be there with you. You know, for support. I might have a hard time if he goes off on you—" he smiles faintly, "—but I'll try not to beat him up."

My chest fills with warmth. Goodness, just when I thought I couldn't love him any more.

After jumping to my tiptoes, I wrap my arms around him. I pull myself up and plant a hard kiss on his cheek. "I would never put you through that kind of torture. Plus, if you were there, he would focus entirely on you, because that's the way he sees things. It would be your fault for leading me astray and taking my purity, because he doesn't see me as having my own sexual desires. He would think I was only trying to please you, and I want to take ownership of this whole thing. I'm done being submissive and weak."

His jaw clenches, and he looks away from me. "It really irritates me when you say that."

I frown. "When I say what?"

His expression shutters, and he turns in the direction of the wharf. "Let's go." His tone is curt. "We can talk about this later."

Nervousness churns in my stomach, but I force my feet to stay in place. "No, I want you to tell me why you're mad."

He whips around, and his gaze burns into mine. "I can't stand it when you call yourself weak. You are the most stable person in my life. You've been there when..." He shakes his head. "You've been there when I didn't even want to be around myself. And you were calm and loving, like you always are. That's not weakness. It takes strength to be close to someone when they're falling apart. Strength that I have yet to see in anyone else." He swallows audibly. "You dazzle me."

He lowers his head and kisses me softly. Jesus, help me, I love him so much. How am I going to bear it if he doesn't love me back like I want him to?

By the time he pulls away, my eyes are full of moisture, and I don't care.

"I'm happy you're asserting yourself more," he says with a smile, "and that you're taking the things you want and standing up for yourself. You should get everything you want. Please don't call yourself weak."

"I won't anymore." *I love you.* The words hover on my lips, but I can't let them out yet. Why spoil this moment when it might become one of my last precious memories with him?

Coldness tightens my chest. Oh my gosh, he was right. He was right all along.

Being with him this way has changed everything. I can't go back to how we were before. It would shatter me.

Maybe I do have inner strength, but I need to start caring

for myself. My soft heart isn't capable of living this way any longer. I can't be this close to him with the invisible wall of platonic friendship between us, not when I love him this much.

If he doesn't want to be with me, I have to end our friendship.

Cole

"LOOK," she says after taking a big bite of her bagel. She points to a couple of birds on the sand. "That seagull just stole whatever that little bird was eating. He just came up and swiped it. I told you they were mean."

A grin spreads over my face. "I think the word you used was 'cruel'."

"I was trying really hard to make it sound like my brain was capable of rational thought, and it backfired on me."

"Oh man, you were high as fuck. It was so cute. At one point, you were staring at your foot like you had never seen it before."

She opens her mouth and closes it when a woman approaches our table. It takes me a moment to recognize her, and when I do, my skin tingles with foreboding.

Sophia from the other night in the Uber.

"I'm so sorry to intrude on your date," she says, "but I haven't been able to stop thinking about the...conversation we had a few days ago about the person we both know."

My pulse starts to race. "It's okay," I say to Sophia. "We don't have to talk around it." I look at Livvy. "This is Sophia. She's a friend of my dad's."

Livvy's eyes widen. "Oh."

"Yeah."

Sophia pulls out a chair from our table, and the metal legs screech like bats as they scrape against the concrete. After sitting down, she looks at me probingly. "I promise I'll be quick. I just kind of panicked when I realized you were his son, and there are a few things I should've said that have been weighing on me."

I swallow, my hands growing cold. "Okay."

God, I really don't want to hear any of this, and I would probably tell her that if Livvy weren't here, but I don't want it to look like I blame the women my dad most likely manipulates into sleeping with him.

"I only hung out with your dad the one time, just like I told you. But I really should have explained a little more about how it happened. I was the one who approached him. I was out with my girlfriends, and he was at the bar by himself. We all thought he was a hot older man—" She looks at Livvy, smiling cheekily. "I mean, it's obviously in their genes, right?"

Fuck, Sophia probably thinks Livvy's my girlfriend, even though I tried to take Sophia home a few days ago.

Like father like son.

"And we were all, like, joking around and saying we would call him Daddy and stuff..." She chuckles nervously. "I'm sorry. I know this is really awkward, but I just want you to understand... We made bets about which one of us would get drunk enough to hit on him, and I was the one who finally did at the end of the night. And I mean, I was pretty buzzed, and I think your dad was *really* drunk—"

I lift a hand. "You don't have to defend him."

"No, no. Please let me finish."

I close my mouth and take a deep breath, wishing I could burst out of my skin to escape this conversation.

"So I ended up going home with him, and we did have sex, but after we were done, he was super sad. Like, I'm pretty sure he almost started crying. He told me he was out getting drunk because it was the anniversary of the day his wife told him about her affair."

"What?"

She winces. "Oh shit, I'm sorry. I don't mean to bring up family drama. I just wanted you to know that I'm pretty sure it was a one-time thing for him. He was really sad about his wife. I got the impression he really loves her and regretted what we did."

My hands press against the table. I want to tell this woman to stop talking and go away before I lose my mind. "Sophia." I try to keep my voice soft. "I don't hold you responsible at all, even if you did approach him. The thing is, you have no clue what you're talking about. It was not a one-time thing. He does this all the time, and whatever he told you about an affair was made up. He's a liar."

"Okay." Her posture grows remote, as if she's finally picking up on how unwelcome this conversation is. "I'm really sorry I interrupted you guys."

She quickly leaves, and I look down at my phone, trying to focus myself before I break down and throw it. I flash the screen. 9:34. Where did the time go? God, I just need to be back in bed with Livvy. That's the only real escape I can get right now.

"Cole."

Her sweet voice pulls me out of my head.

"I'm so sorry," she says. "That was awful."

"She didn't tell me anything I didn't already know."

"No, that was traumatizing. I can't even imagine having to hear stuff like that about my parents. I understand what she was trying to do, but oh my gosh, why did she have to go into so much detail?"

I nod slowly. God, I don't think I've ever hated my dad

more. How could he use my mom like that, pretending to be sad to get women to sleep with him? Isn't it enough that she's stood by his side all these years while he's fucked other women, some of them in my mom's own home?

I'm never getting married.

"What?"

When I jerk up at the sound of her voice, her brows are drawn together, and her mouth is tight. Fuck, I must have mumbled that.

I clear my throat. "I just fucking hate my dad."

She purses her lips as she nods. "Do you want to head home now?" Her voice is tight.

Home.

I get to take her home with me.

I get to keep her there for a while—the only person in the world who makes me feel safe and warm.

I'm never letting her go.

Oh God, these feelings are dangerous. I can't have her this close forever. Ultimately it will drive her away.

I have to make the most of the short time we have.

"Yeah, let's get of here." I force a smile. "We have unfinished business."

SIXTEEN

Livvy

I RUN my palms over the skirt of my dress. The white nylon fabric is unwrinkled—pristine, just like my pure little life.

I hope he dirties it by the end of the night.

Just before I turn around and walk out of the bathroom, I grab the silver ring from the counter and slip it onto my finger.

In just a few minutes, everything this ring represents will be gone.

I smile as I walk out of the bathroom and into Cole's bedroom. When he looks up from his phone, he smiles warmly. Thank God, he's come out of his somber mood.

I'll think about his marriage comment later. I already knew he was scared of commitment. It doesn't necessarily mean he won't take the risk of being in a relationship with me, especially if the next hour is as spectacular as I think it could be.

"You're wearing white," he says.

"Yeah, I want to recreate all the things I always planned to do on my first time, except I want it way, way filthier. I probably would have worn white lingerie on my wedding night, but this was the best I could do on short notice." I lift my hand in the air. "I'm also wearing my purity ring. I would have given it to my husband before we had sex, but I think I'd rather wear it. It seems dirtier to have it on while you're railing me."

He chuckles softly, shaking his head. "This is so fucked up."

"You think so? Purity culture isn't really Biblical, so it doesn't feel like blasphemy to me, but we don't need to do it like this if it creeps you out."

"It doesn't. You're just so different than I thought you would be." His smile grows lazy. "You're kind of a little freak."

"Only because you make me so comfortable." After I plop down on the bed, I plant a kiss on his cheek. "Okay, I have one more thing to show you, and you're going to die laughing." I reach into the pocket of my dress and pull out the tattered paper. "I wrote a letter to my future husband when I was thirteen, and I want to read it to you."

"Oh my God."

I laugh. "I know. Just wait till you hear it. I spent so much time trying to word it eloquently, and it's so basic. It also took me probably an hour to make all of my letters perfect, because I wanted it to look really pretty for my husband."

"That's kind of sweet."

"Oh, it is. So sweet and *so* sad. Okay..." I take a deep breath as my gaze drops to the calligraphy letters. "'Dear Future Husband. Today I made a promise to God that I would wait for you. I'm saving my first kiss and my first everything...'" I giggle. "Isn't it so sad that I had to say 'everything' instead of 'sex'? I couldn't even write out the thing I was promising to save. Okay, I need to skip some of this because it's a bunch of evangelical jargon. Oh, this is the best part right here. The ending. 'I pray that you will wait for me too, but it's okay if you don't. You might be on a different journey than me, and I trust in God's plan. No matter what happens in your life before we come together, know that I already love you with all of my heart, and I will love you forever."

I let the paper fall to my lap, heat enveloping my chest. "It's so embarrassing. Could there be any less sexy foreplay?"

When Cole stays silent, I turn to him. His brows are drawn together, and his gaze is unfocused. "I think it's really sweet," he finally says.

What is this shift in his mood? He looks more like he did an hour ago after that wretched conversation at the coffee shop.

"Sort of, but I didn't really know what I was saying. All of these letters are very similar, because our youth pastors usually guide us on what to say. Most of the girls at my church wrote something like this."

"Yeah, but I bet you really meant it. It's very like you to love someone without them having to earn it, and to stick by them no matter what."

I nod slowly. There's no reason to tell him that I don't think that part of me was ever healthy, or that I'm glad it's starting to change. He's clearly touched by my letter, and I don't want to spoil the mood.

I'm startled when he grabs me by the shoulders and presses a hard kiss against my lips. His mouth moves to my jaw, and he starts trailing it down my neck. "You're an angel," he whispers against my skin.

"Mmm." The bedroom version of his usual endearment is so much better than the earnest one. "That feels good."

When his mouth returns to mine, he immediately slips his tongue inside. His kiss is frantic—almost desperate—as if he's searching for something. When he sucks my lip into his mouth and bites down, I gasp. He stiffens before pulling away.

My gaze falls to his rapidly moving chest. "Sorry," he says breathlessly. He turns away and runs both hands through his hair. "I've wanted this for five years. I think I'm losing my mind now that I'm about to get it. We might need to take breaks."

"Cole, no. I don't want you to stop yourself. I want you unhinged, like you were last night."

He smiles warmly. "We can be rough after you've gotten used to sex, but not right now. I could hurt you."

"I want you to be rough."

He sighs heavily. "It was different last night. My tongue couldn't hurt you."

"Believe me when I say I want it to be rough. I don't even mind if it hurts. I actually kind of liked it when you bit me. I want it to be filthy and rough and a little painful." I place my hands on his cheeks and stare into those dark brown eyes. "I want you to make me impure."

Something ignites behind his eyes. He grips me by the hair and yanks my head back, sending a tingling pain into my scalp. After pressing a soft kiss against my neck, he bites down softly. Heat coils in my belly.

"Is this what you want?" The words are delivered through clenched teeth.

"Yes," I gasp.

He grips my hair tighter. "You need to tell me if I hurt you too much. I won't do this if you're going to pretend everything's fine when you're in pain."

"I won't."

"I don't believe you. I think you'll see how turned on I am, and you won't want to spoil the moment for me. I won't be rough with you unless you swear to God you'll stop me if I really hurt you, and I mean that literally. Swear to your God right now."

I frown. "Could I promise to God instead? I don't believe in swearing to God."

When his eyes grow wide, my face heats. Goodness, he probably thinks I'm so childish. "I know it's just semantics..." My voice is faint.

"It's okay." He loosens his grip on my hair as he presses a gentle kiss against my cheek. "Promise to God, then."

I meet his heavy-lidded gaze. "I promise to God that I'll tell you if you hurt me too much."

"Good girl." His eyes grow fierce. He yanks me back onto the bed. The burning pain in my scalp warms my whole body.

"That didn't hurt?" he asks.

"It hurt, but I liked it."

He groans as he crawls on top of me and settles his weight over my body. Wow, he's heavy, and his chest is as hard as concrete.

"Filthy girl," he says. "Do you want my cock now?"

"Yes," I whisper.

He grips my chin. "Beg for it."

Heat prickles over my skin. I open my mouth and close it. Why is it so hard to talk this way when I love it when he does it?

He laughs softly. "You can do it, Angel. Be a good girl and beg for my cock."

I avert my gaze from his. "Please give me your—" I lower my voice, "—cock."

"That was good, but I want you to say it louder. Say 'Cole, I want your cock'."

A jolt of heat shoots into my groin. Why is it so much hotter when he says it? With effort, I raise my voice. "Cole, I want your cock."

"Are you wet for me?"

I swallow. "Yeah."

"Take that off now," he says, pointing to my dress. "And look at me while you do it."

My face heats, but I don't hesitate. His eyelids grow lazy as I lift the skirt of my dress to my chest. When I pull it over my head and expose my breasts to the air in the room, cold shame starts to coil in my stomach, but it vanishes the moment I look at his possessive gaze.

"Underwear too. Now. And spread your legs open when you're done. I want to look at you."

I grab the elastic at my hips. Even as nervous as I am, I'm able to pull my panties down slowly and enjoy the darkening of his expression. After I toss them on the floor, I open my legs.

The little sound he makes is almost a whimper. He doesn't move for a moment, and the silence in the room grows thick as he stares between my legs. Shame starts to tingle over my skin, and I can't help but drop my gaze to the carpet.

"No." His voice is hard. "Look at me now, or I'll spank you."

My stomach flips over. Oh my God, I never thought I would want something like that. It was humiliating being spanked by my parents. Why is the thought of being bent over his lap making electricity shoot through my veins?

"I caught you," he says. "You have to follow my rules now."

All my instincts tell me to look at him, even though I want to be spanked. I keep my gaze fixed on the carpet, and my cheeks fill with heat. I never disobeyed my parents on purpose. Even playful disobedience feels extremely naughty.

"Alright." In my periphery, I see him march in my direction. "Time to be punished."

In an instant, my belly is set on top of his hard thighs. His warm hand brushes over my bare butt, and heat fills my gut.

"Oh fuck, Livvy. You have such a beautiful ass. I've wanted to touch it for so long."

I grin. "I bet you wanted to spank me two nights ago when I ran off."

He laughs. "I did. If you'd only told me I could, my resolve would have vanished. I'd have fucked you then and there."

I hum. "I want you to fuck me now."

"No." His voice is rough. "You've been naughty."

The sound of his slap echoes across the room. The sting sets in a few seconds later, like tiny needles pricking my skin. Jesus, help me, his hand felt stronger than wood. I guess I shouldn't be surprised. He is a pitcher.

"Wow." I gasp.

He smooths his warm palm over my butt. "Are you okay, baby?"

"Yeah." I gulp in a deep breath to ease the pain. "I don't think my parents ever even spanked me that hard."

"Oh shit. Am I traumatizing you by doing this?"

"No," I say quickly. "I really like it. I think I like pain."

"Hearing you say things like that is like a fever dream." His voice drops low. "You're going to get a lot of it. I'm going to spank you more, and then I'm going to shove my cock into your tight pussy. You're going to take it like a good girl. Do you understand?"

I whimper. "Yes."

The pressure of his hand settles on my lower back. "If you move at all while I spank you, you're getting fucked right away, and I won't be gentle."

My vision turns into slits. "Okay."

A hard slap resounds, and this time the sharp pain makes my gut clench. I wiggle a little, just so I can get the punishment I crave.

He holds me tightly. "Looks like you want my cock."

His big fingers squeeze into my waist as he flips my back onto the bed. After settling his hard body over mine, he grabs my wrists and pins them over my head. He's so heavy, I can hardly take in a breath. "I'm going to hold you like this," he says, "so you know you can't get away, but then I'm going to be gentle with you." He presses soft kisses from my jaw to my collarbone. "Like this." He talks between kisses. "Because I can't just hurt you. You're too sweet. Even when you're naughty, I want to make you feel good."

I swallow. "But you are going to hurt me. You're going to shove your cock inside of me."

His groan is almost a growl. "It'll only hurt at first." When he sucks my nipple into his mouth, I whimper. "But then I'm going to make you feel so good. I want to keep you. I won't let you go but I don't want you to run away from me again."

A smile tugs at my lips. I love that he knows exactly what to say in my private fantasy world.

"What happens if I try to run away?"

With one hand wrapped around my wrists, he sets the other on the back of my head and brushes his fingers against my scalp. My eyelids fall shut, and when he grips my hair and yanks my head back, I gasp.

"You'll get punished. That way you'll understand you're mine now." He lets go of my hair and sets two fingers on my clit.

I thrust my hips forward. "Yes!" The word is a plea.

"I won't let you go, Angel, but I'm going to make you feel so good that you'll want to stay with me forever."

When he starts rubbing my clit, I whimper.

"You're going to beg me to stick my cock in you."

"Yes! Please, Cole."

"Not yet." He rubs faster. "Is this how you like it?"

I shift back from his hard fingers, trying to find my rhythm. "A little softer."

He eases his touch to a little more than a tickle, and it's

perfect. Electricity spreads from my core to the tips of my fingers and toes. "Of course," he whispers into my ear, "you're soft. Soft and sweet like an angel, and I've wanted to soil you from the moment I laid eyes on you."

"Cole!"

He lets go of my wrists and places a palm over my mouth, pressing down hard. "Not now. Only when you come."

I moan, and the sound is muffled against his hand. Abruptly, he withdraws his hand from my clit, and my hips jerk at the loss of his touch.

"I'm going to fuck you now." His eyes are nearly shut.

"Yes."

As he gets up to undress himself, I look away for a moment, nervousness starting to flutter over my skin. The sound of plastic ripping open makes my whole stomach flip over. That must be the condom.

This is really happening. In a moment, I won't be pure anymore.

Cole

I'M NEVER LETTING her go.

Those soft brown eyes stare up at me as I grab my cock and place it between her legs. As I start to work my way inside, a warm wave washes over me, making me dizzy. "Oh Christ, you're tight."

"Too tight?" As soon as the words are out, she winces and turns her head. "Sorry. What a virgin thing to say."

Oh God, she's sweet.

And all mine.

I grab her by the chin, gritting my teeth as she clenches

around me. "You're perfectly tight, but you're still going to take all of me, Angel. Do you understand?"

Her eyelids grow heavy. "Yes, Cole."

When I push myself all the way inside, I let out the groan I'd been holding in. It sounds like a roar to my ears.

It's only when I start to move that a shred of humanity pulls me out of my primitive sexual haze. I glance down at her, and those pretty dark brows are drawn together.

I place my hand on her cheek. "Oh Livvy, baby. I forgot to ask you if it hurts."

She shakes her head. "It doesn't."

After running my fingers from the back of her neck to her scalp, I grip her tightly by the hair. "Tell me the truth, Angel. You promised to God you would."

"It's just a little uncomfortable, but it's already going away, and I don't want you to stop. I want you to call me a good girl again."

Tenderness tightens my chest. "You are a good girl, taking my whole cock."

When she stares up at me with those big, beautiful eyes—full of awe and trust—I lose myself. Here she is, my angel. I caught her, and now that I have her by the hair with my cock deep inside her, I'm never letting her go.

I'll be good to her, but I won't let her go.

"I'm going to mark you," I say. "So that everyone knows you're mine."

"Okay..." It sounds like a question.

I lean forward and lick her neck before biting down. She hisses, but I don't think I really hurt her. I pull away and look down, loving the red print on her pretty skin.

"If anyone asks you about that, say Cole gave it to you." I grab her hips before thrusting hard. "Because I own you now."

She whimpers, nodding frantically. "Yes!"

"I own every part of you." I grip her by the neck and squeeze tightly. "Say it. Say, 'Cole, you own me'."

She thrusts against me, clearly trying to find her own rhythm, but I won't let her. Not until she gives me what I want. "Cole, you..."

I give her neck a squeeze. "Say I own you. Say it!"

"You own me."

Her words flow through me like a drug, and my eyes fall shut. I ram into her tightness again and again, clenching my teeth to keep the unbearable pleasure from sending me over the edge. I need more. So much more.

"All of you," I say, as I trail my fingers down her big, luscious ass. I slip one finger between her cheeks and press it into her tight hole.

She shrieks, and I laugh. "That's mine too," I say. "Every part of you. Oh God, Livvy, I'm going to fuck all of it. Fuck you raw." I pound into her so hard that her head presses into the wall.

"Cole!"

"Yeah, you like that, don't you? Filthy girl. My fallen angel."

"Yes!"

Her dazed eyes tell me she's close to coming, so I place my hand on her skin and trail it down until I find her clit. I rub softly up and down, and she releases a soft little whimper. Her pussy clenches around my cock. The pleasure is so overwhelming, I could die.

When I slam into her again, she stares up at me with her brow furrowed and her lips parted.

It's the look.

The look that makes me feel like a hero and a dark villain at the same time. A look that stirs ancient feelings of subduing and conquering.

When I remove my hand from her clit, her eyes widen. "Cole?"

She's sexually frustrated, and God, I shouldn't be doing this. This should be about her pleasure only.

But I can't help myself.

"Tell me you're mine forever," I whisper into her ear. "And I'll let you come."

"You're..." I pound into her, she intakes a sharp breath. "You're mine."

"No." I grip her shoulders and dig my fingers into her skin. "Say, 'Cole, I'm yours forever'."

She whimpers. "Cole, I'm yours forever."

Pleasure radiates throughout my body. I'm so close to coming. I have to grit my teeth to fight it. I place my fingers on her clit and rub slowly.

"Yes!"

I increase the pace of my fingers, and each thrust into her sends spasms of heat throughout my body. "Say it again."

Her brows draw together. "Say what?"

"Say, 'I'm yours forever'."

"I'm yours forever!" This time, she shouts and moans as her body flails every which way.

"Yeah, that's it. Come for me, baby." When I increase my pace, she screams. She clenches around my cock in pulses, her eyelids falling nearly shut.

"Oh fuck, you're so gorgeous," I say.

Just as her body grows limp, I pull out of her and yank off the condom. "You're going to take all of my come."

I put my hand around my cock. After only one stroke, electricity shoots from my core and pulses through my veins. Fuck, this is the most unbearable pleasure of my life. Come spurts out of my cock onto her belly, and a dark possessiveness settles over me.

She's mine.

My mind is blank for a few blissful moments. It's just me and the soft angel in my arms. The voice of regret is so distant now, it's hardly a mutter.

But as the seconds pass, and the post-orgasm bliss starts to fade, and the voice gets closer.

This was only her first time, and she has her whole life ahead of her.

She's not really yours forever.

SEVENTEEN

Livvy

"OH MY GOODNESS. THAT WAS WILD."

He smiles faintly.

"I'm so glad it was like that. Thank you for making my first time so special. Doing it like that was healing for me."

"Of course, baby."

He lies still with his eyes closed, looking thoroughly sated. I should just let him rest, but I can't. Elation is making me bold, and I won't let this opportunity pass.

"I think we're good together. Our friendship means we have really good communication, and that leads to explosive sex." My insides quiver, but I have to press forward.

It's time to face my fears.

"I want more. I don't want to go back to being just friends after this week."

His eyes pop open. He opens his mouth and closes it. My

stomach plummets, but I try to push away the ominous feeling taking over my body.

This is okay. He's just surprised.

"Livvy…"

When he doesn't say anything more, my head grows unsteady. Could I have misinterpreted everything? "I mean, maybe… Was it just me? Did I think it was really good sex because of my lack of experience?"

"No. God, no." After reaching out and grabbing my hand, his gaze falls to the sticky wetness on my belly, and he smiles faintly. "I wouldn't have done that if I hadn't completely lost my head. You're right. It was explosive sex. Let me get a towel so I can clean you up."

When he stands up and disappears from the room, my chest constricts. Is this deflection? Is he trying to change the subject?

Boldness, Livvy. Boldness.

"Well, if it was spectacular for you too," I call out, "then it's probably only going to get better. Why would we stop in a week?"

The faucet shuts off, and he walks back into the bedroom. His grim expression makes a ball of ice form in the pit of my stomach. He kneels in front of the bed and presses a warm cloth against my skin, rubbing softly.

"Why aren't you saying anything?"

His jaw ticks. "I'm thinking."

"Obviously, your thoughts aren't positive. I can see it all over your face."

After pushing himself up, he walks over to his closet and reaches to the top shelf. He pulls out a baseball and stares at it for a moment before tossing it into the air and catching it. He does it again and again.

My head jerks back. "Are we going to play catch before we finish this conversation?"

"I told you I'm thinking."

My breathing grows shallow, and I shut my eyes to fight the dizziness. This isn't good. He hardly even seems aware of his movements.

"Why is it so hard to give this idea a chance?" I ask.

After catching the ball, he pauses for a moment. He steps to the side and lifts his elbow high in the air, like he's going to pitch, but he only tosses the ball softly onto the bed. "You're asking me to choose between friendship and sex."

"That's not what I'm asking at all. We'll still be friends."

"For now." His voice is so faint.

Heat creeps along my neck and into my cheeks. "So you're just not willing to take the risk that we might break up someday? I guess what I feel for you is much stronger than what you feel for me."

"No." He whips around to face me. "The opposite of that is true. I could never risk losing you. The only way I would even consider this is if you could guarantee that we would still be friends for the rest of our lives even if we try and it doesn't work out. Can you guarantee that?"

His slight smile is almost a sneer. He knows I won't lie.

"No, I can't."

"Of course you can't. Friendship is a guarantee. A romantic relationships isn't. I don't even believe in monogamy."

My ears pound like a hammer. Jesus, help me, I wonder how many times he's made this exact speech right after sex. "That's a fuck-boy thing to say."

The swearword on my lips must sound as strange to him as it did to me, because his eyes grow huge. He stares at me for a moment as if he's never seen me before. "You're calling me a fuck-boy because I care about you too much to lose you?"

I cross my arms over my chest. "The fact that you talk about losing me like it's a sure thing tells me you don't really want me. You already see yourself dumping me when we haven't even started anything yet."

"That's not true at all. I can't see the future, and that's the problem. All I know is that passion doesn't last. We had sex, and it was great, but our friendship is so much more. How can you not see that?"

My throat aches, and I struggle to swallow. I'm not going to win this battle. He's determined to keep things as they were.

Because he doesn't want me enough.

"So if you want to go back to being just friends," I say, "I guess that means you don't mind if I start having sex with other guys, because I'm certainly not staying celibate after this."

His look of horror would be comical if I weren't so close to tears.

"Did that not even occur to you?" I ask. "Do you think going back to our old friendship means I'll go back to being the old me?"

He averts his gaze from mine, his nostrils flaring.

"Did you think that I would be this person forever—sweet, compassionate Livvy who's always there for you at the drop of a hat because she has nothing else going on in her life?"

When his eyes grow wide and dazed, I huff softly. He did think I would always be this way, because this is who I've always been—devoted to him, even when he's slept with other women. In a way, I have been his girlfriend. He just got sex elsewhere.

"I think our relationship is a little enmeshed," I say.

His gaze snaps to my face. "What do you mean?"

"I mean it's unhealthy. Relationships are supposed to grow. You want to keep me in a box, and maybe it's because you treasure me, but it's not doing me any favors. You're part of the reason I've lived so small."

His mouth drops open. "I don't want you to live small. I'm happy to see you grow and—"

"No." I shake my head sharply. "You're happy to see me grow as long as who I grow into suits you. As long as I don't grow away from you, and you get to call all the shots. I've basically been your girlfriend for all these years, all while you got to sleep with countless other women, but you would hate it if I slept with other guys. And you know you'll try to intervene in the name of 'protectiveness'."

His nostrils flare, but he wisely doesn't speak. We both know any kind of denial would be a lie.

"In many ways, I've been submissive to you, just like I was taught to be with my husband someday. I know you love and care for me, but you want things your way. I've been on hold for you all these years, and you want to put me on hold again."

He scowls. "What do you mean by 'on hold'? Being with you wasn't even an option until a few days ago."

"No." I stare at him steadily. Dread clamps my chest like a fist, and I take a deep breath to ease it as much as I can.

Now is the time.

The entirety of our friendship has led to this moment. As long as I keep my love a secret, I can live in the fantasy world that he loves me and doesn't know it. The delusion has been a shelter for my pathetic heart. At the back of my mind, I've always known that once it crumbles, my heart will too.

But I'm ready for that.

"Cole, I'm in love with you. I always have been."

Cole

. . .

THERE'S a roar in my head. "Always? You mean since we first met?"

Her brows draw together. "Yes. I fell in love with you during those first few months we were getting to know each other."

The world around me starts to blur, and my body grows so light I could float away. I see her as she was back then—my beautiful Livvy who wore modest clothes and never cursed. How could she have been in love with me? "But you only liked Christian guys back then."

She stares at me for a moment. "You seem to think that because I'm religious, I'm a different species than you. You know that I'm not really an angel, right? Even before I decided to break out of purity culture, I had human desires like everyone else. I wanted you. I was crazy horny for you, but it very quickly became much deeper than that." Her voice grows hushed. "I fell in love with your heart. You made me see that people can be good without Jesus. My faith might never have evolved if not for you."

My chest seizes, and I avert my gaze from hers. Oh God, she really loves me. How is this happening? Am I in heaven? "So...you loved me as I was back then?" I exhale a shaky breath. "You didn't want me to change?"

"It was so much deeper than that. I thought you were designed for me by God. There was no way I could love you so much if you weren't going to become a Christian someday, but I didn't really think it would change you. You were already everything I wanted, just by being you."

I nod slowly as adrenaline pulses through my veins. Oh God, if only I had known this during my last few weeks at that church. Those were some of the most miserable days of my life. That was when I finally realized that I could never be with her. I would have fallen into despair if I hadn't rationalized my way out of it. I still had her. Maybe I couldn't get everything I wanted, but I got enough to sustain myself, and what I had was a sure thing. She would never abandon me as long as we were just friends.

I held on to that comfort so fiercely that I refused to see it for what it really was—a delusion that provided a shield for the true despair.

The despair of believing her feelings would never match mine. How could they when I had so much evidence to the contrary? I loved her from the moment I met her, just as she is, but she wouldn't even consider me unless I completely transformed. I was cursed to live like my mom, waiting for someone to love me when they never would, at least not in the way that I needed.

Oh God, I've been so wrong.

And so stupid.

"As you can see," she says, "I've been on hold for you for many years."

"Why did you never say anything?" My voice is a croak.

"As long as I kept it a secret, I could lie to myself that eventually you would realize you love me too." She glances down at the crumpled blanket on the bed and smooths it out with her palm. "But I'm not that weak anymore. I don't need to lie to myself." She meets my gaze. "I'm done waiting for you. You made your choice, and it doesn't work for me. We can't be just friends anymore."

A buzzing sounds in my ears. Her face shifts for a moment, like she's someone else. This can't really be happening. She couldn't have really said that.

"Um..." My head grows heavy. I shut my eyes for a moment to fight the dizziness. "What?"

Her brow furrows. "Oh, Cole. I know this is really hard for you. I'm so sorry."

Holy fuck, is she comforting me? Did she just take away my entire world and tell me she's sorry that I'm alone now?

"Livvy," I say, my voice shaky. "Are you really saying what I think you're saying?"

Her eyes grow glassy. "I have to do what's best for me, as much as it breaks my heart. Going back to our old friendship would break my heart every day." Her voice cracks, and she inhales an unsteady breath. I walk over to the bed and hold out my arms, but she lifts both hands. "No, I can't be touched by you right now."

"Livvy..." It's a plea.

"You'll be okay."

Several tears fall down her cheeks, and I wish I could lift them back into her eyes. Why can't we go back to five minutes ago, before we said words that changed everything?

"We'll both be okay," she says.

"No, I won't!"

"You will. It'll be hard at first but healthier for both of us in the long run. You're too dependent on me emotionally, and I'm too much of a doormat with you."

"You're not a doormat! You own me. If you want a relationship, you can have it. You can have anything you want. I'll worship you for the rest of my life. If I had any idea I was going to lose you, I would have said that from the beginning."

Her lips quiver as she nods. "That's the problem. Our relationship is whatever suits you best in the moment. You want to keep me in your life, and you're willing to do something you don't want to do—"

"I do want it!" My throat constricts, and I swallow to ease it. "I love you. I've been madly in love with you since the day we met."

She purses her lips, not looking at all affected by my confession, and it makes me want to burst out of my skin.

"Cole, you're saying that in a moment of desperation."

I inhale a deep, shaky breath, trying to get my rapid heart-beat under control. "Yes, I'm desperate, but it's also true. I promise you it's true. I've been in denial about it. It was the only way I could keep you in my life without wanting to die for never being able to really have you."

"You can really have me, though." Her voice is brittle. "You just did, and you rejected me immediately afterward. My heart is broken. If you supposedly feel the same way, how can you not understand that?"

I raise both hands in the air. "I'm a fucking idiot! I was just scared that I might lose you. If not now, maybe a few months from now...or years...and that's fucking terrifying!"

Her lips purse. "I was scared too, but not too scared to take the risk. Not after what we just shared."

Oh God, she said something like that a few days ago. *"You can't have real love without risk."* How the fuck am I going to make her believe me?

"Livvy, please..." My voice cracks. "You're my entire world, and it feels like that world is ending right now..."

Her eyes are full of compassion, as they usually are when I'm upset, but she hasn't touched me once. She hasn't set her hand on my arm and squeezed it.

Oh God, she's already leaving me. She's already fading away, like if I reached out in touched her, my hand would sink through.

"It isn't healthy for me to be your entire world, and what good does it do me if you aren't willing to truly be with me?"

"I am!" I hate how desperate I sound.

"Because you see it as your only option." She takes a shaky breath. "But it's not even that."

"Oh God, Livvy." A trickle runs down my cheek. "Please..."

My throat closes over. *Please don't leave me. I'll do anything to keep you.*

"I'm so sorry." Our gazes hold for a moment before her expression grows remote. She glances around the room. "I need to leave before I break down. Would you mind turning around while I get dressed?"

I stare at her for a moment, her words not computing. Why do I need to turn around?

Oh my God, in the span of minutes, I've lost the right to see her naked. I had everything a moment ago, and it's gone now.

By doing everything in my power to keep her in my life, I lost her.

I nod slowly before turning around, and it's like the lights shut off in my head. The next thing I know, she's saying goodbye with that gray duffel bag at her side, and I'm nodding in response, unable to speak. She disappears from my room and the front door shuts, but the sound is coming from faraway.

The walls of my room become close and oppressive. I have to get out of here. I glance at the baseball on the bed, and in the next moment, it's flying into the window, shattering the glass.

LIVVY

THE DRIVEWAY IS empty when I pull into it. Thank God, my parents are gone, but hopefully Vanessa is home. I allow myself one last heaving sob before taking a deep breath and stepping out of the car.

I did everything right. I asked for what I wanted and stood up for myself when I didn't get it, and that's something to be proud of.

The despair will fade. This ache in my chest is a physical

pain, and I want to rush back to his house to ease it. I want to wrap my arms around him and tell him I'll take whatever I can get, but those are just fleeting emotions and desires.

My will is stronger than they are.

I rush inside the house and up the stairs. Vanessa's bedroom door is shut, which is a good sign she's home. I only have to knock twice before she opens it.

"What happened?" she asks.

I can't talk about it with her yet. "Do you have a lighter?"

Her brows draw together. "I have a stick lighter for my candles."

"Grab it and meet me in the backyard."

She stares at me a moment before nodding. I reach into my bag, sifting my hand around until I find the frayed paper at the top.

Minutes later, we're both out on the back porch. I unfold the letter to my future husband and stare it for a moment. Something about the curling letters causes my eyes to prickle. Thirteen-year-old me tried so hard to make this as pretty as I could, because it meant something to me. I loved it. I love it even now, and there's something hauntingly melancholy about loving something that I was coerced into believing, something I didn't even understand.

"I'm guessing it didn't go well..." Vanessa's soft voice pulls me out of my head.

"No."

After nodding faintly, she looks away. She'd never say anything resembling "I told you so" because she's far too empathetic, and she knows how deeply troubled I am, but she's thinking it. She's thinking this is why girls should save themselves for their husbands. This is why sex before marriage is wrong. When you step outside of the boundaries, you only get hurt. I thought the same things at her age.

I want to tell her that nothing can protect her from heartache, not even God. I want to tell her that all the methods she's using to guard her heart and purity may one day become their own source of pain and grief and guilt. Instead, I light the stick lighter and hold it to my letter.

It takes a moment to catch. A small flame forms and spreads, traveling slowly upward. The fire and ash twist and curl, dancing around the paper as they pull it into oblivion. Before the heat reaches my fingers, I toss the small remains on the concrete and stomp on it.

"There," I say. "I'm done with purity culture, and I'm done with Cole. My future is unwritten, and that's exciting."

"Is it?" Vanessa asks, looking a little bewildered, probably because I'm acting so strangely.

"No." I sigh. "Not at the moment, but I have hope."

EIGHTEEN

Cole

THE WORLD IS DARK AGAIN, just like it was years ago before she came into my life.

I'd almost forgotten what this feels like. A dust cloud has swept over everything, and yet it all looks exactly the same. She left her water glass on my dresser, and even from here I can make out a little pink smudge on the edge from her lip gloss. Her white dress sits crumpled on the floor, in the same place she left it after she slipped it over her head.

I can't disturb any of it. It's as if I can pull her back into my life by preserving the world as it was just before I lost her.

Fuck, I need to get out of this room.

When I step outside, the afternoon sun is high in the sky and relentlessly bright. If things had gone differently, if I hadn't been so selfish and shortsighted, I probably wouldn't even know the time right now. I'd be in bed with her in my room, and we'd be speaking as softly as if it were the dead of night.

As soon as I get inside my parent's house, I walk into the kitchen. What the fuck am I even doing here? I can't eat or drink anything right now.

"Honey, what's wrong?" When I glance up, my mom is sitting at the kitchen table. Fuck, how did I not even see her? I forgot she was due back today. Her expression fills with alarm as she strides in my direction. She sets her hand on my forehead. "Are you sick?"

"No, I'm fine," I say, though my voice is as husky as when I have a cold.

"No, you're not." She scans my face. "Have you been crying?" Her eyes widen as if a thought occurs to her. "Are you upset about the divorce?"

"No, it has nothing to do with that. Everything's fine. I'm just tired, but I did..."

God, I can't believe I have to tell her I did the exact same thing her piece of shit husband did a few days ago.

"I broke a window in the guesthouse."

Her head jerks back. "What happened?"

I sigh heavily, shutting my eyes. "It was an accident, but I cleaned everything up. I'm going to get it replaced as soon as I can, and when I get my first paycheck, I'll get that whole place deep cleaned for you."

She stares at me for a long moment. "Why do I think it wasn't an accident? Tell me what's going on."

"I don't want to unload on you, not with everything you're going through with Dad."

"You'll be doing me a favor by unloading on me. If you don't, I'll worry."

In the end, I tell her the story because I'm too exhausted to argue with her. With each detail I share, the tension leaves my shoulders, and based on her concerned but placid expression, my mom is isn't disturbed by any of it.

"I wasn't in a rage when I threw the ball," I say when I'm finished. "I was honestly just... I don't know... I hardly even remember throwing it."

"You were in shock."

"I guess so."

She nods slowly, her brow furrowed.

"What are you thinking?" I ask.

"I'm just surprised you didn't want to be in a relationship with her. Whenever you used to say you don't do relationships, I always thought it was because you couldn't be with her. Because her religion is so strict."

I huff, shaking my head. "I'm a fucking idiot, Mom. I guess she just took me by surprise, and I freaked out. It's so stupid. Now I have nothing."

Her expression grows stern. "You need to talk to her."

"She's been gone three hours, and I've already called her twenty times." I laugh humorlessly. "I think she turned off her phone, because it's going straight to voice mail now."

"Well, you'd better find a way to see her whenever she's ready. You can't let it go and hope that she comes around. This needs to be dealt with now, unless you want to lose her for good."

The sound pulled from my chest is something between a groan and a cry. If I can't get her back, I'll be forced to live in this dark and desolate world forever.

My stomach jolts when a thought occurs to me. "She left a few of her things at the house. Would it seem manipulative if I brought them to her and asked to talk to her?"

She stares at me for a moment. "Maybe wait a week or so. Give her a little bit of space first."

I nod frantically, even though I have no intention of waiting even close to a week. I don't think I'm physically capable of it.

I'll wait until tomorrow. Any longer, and I'll lose my mind.

. . .

LIVVY

I SCRUB the sponge against the glass plate so hard that it slips out of my hand. I catch it just before it hits the bottom of the sink.

Goodness, I need an outlet for all of this nervous energy. I wish I liked running.

"Livvy." My sister raises her voice over the faucet water.

I turn it off before twisting around. "What's up?"

Something about her wary expression makes the back of my neck prickle. "Cole is outside. In his car."

My stomach flutters, and I hate myself for it.

"He doesn't want to come to the door because he doesn't want to cause a scene with Mom and Dad around, so he DMed me on Instagram. He said you're not responding to his texts."

My throat grows tight. I haven't even looked at his texts. I've been too terrified that I might slip back into being passive Livvy and tell him I take everything back.

"He has a bunch of your stuff that you left at his house," Vanessa says. "I didn't bring it in, because he asked if he could talk to you."

My spine grows rigid. "I can't. It's too soon. I'm too raw."

"I understand, but like..." Her eyes widen. "Livvy, he looks...like he's sick. I think he's really devastated about whatever happened with you guys."

My heart squeezes, and I wish I could hug him. Why do I still have these instincts? Why do I want to comfort him when he's the one who broke my heart?

Enough. I don't need to comfort him, and I'm not too weak to see him.

I brush past my sister in the direction of the front door, taking several deep breaths to calm my racing heart. By the time I make it outside, my resolve is a little firmer.

I'm not going to talk to him today. We'll have a heart-to-heart when I'm strong enough to put my needs above his.

He steps out of his car as soon I get close, and my sister was right. Jesus, help me, he looks awful. His eyes are dull, and his skin is bleached of color.

He clears his throat. "You left your dress and...I think maybe mascara or something. I didn't want to bring them to the door with your parents at home."

I nod. "My sister told me, but that's not really why you came over."

"No." His voice is soft. "I was hoping we could talk."

I take a deep breath. I can do this. "Not right now. It's too soon."

"This is hell." His voice quivers.

Moisture starts to gather in my eyes. "I know. It's not easy for me either."

"When can I come back?"

I sigh. "I'll text you when I'm ready. We can meet somewhere and talk everything out."

When his face lights up, I lift a hand. "We're just going to have a conversation. I'll let you talk, because I know I left abruptly yesterday, but I really don't anticipate anything changing between us."

When his shoulders slump a little and his expression grows remote, I wish I could reach and touch him.

"That's understandable." His voice is so faint, I only just make it out.

When his eyes grow bright and misty, I walk quickly in his direction and reach for the paper bag in his hands.

I need to get away fast. His despair is squeezing my resolve into dust.

As I grip the handle of the bag, his thumb brushes over my hand, and just that small touch sends an electrical current up my arm. When I look up at him, his gaze is boring into mine, his expression so full of longing my heart falls into my stomach.

I turn around and walk quickly into the house.

When I make it to the staircase, Vanessa approaches me. "Dad is pissed," she mouths.

My brow knits, and a moment later, my dad walks out of the kitchen. "What's in that bag?" His tone is full of accusation.

I'm too emotionally exhausted to lie. "A dress and a tube of eyeliner."

"Why did Cole have them?"

"He picked them up from Mari's friend's house," Vanessa says quickly. My heart clenches that she's trying to cover for me even when I don't really need it.

I'm done behaving like a child.

My dad keeps his gaze fixed on me. "I don't think that's where she really went. Why have I never heard of this Brenna until now? And why did you come home early?" He shakes his head. "I think you stayed at Cole's house."

My last nerve snapping, I lift my chin and stare up at my dad. "It's none of your business if I did."

"So this is how it is now? Staying overnight with men." His nostrils flare. "I never saw this coming. I don't know where my daughter went."

I grit my teeth. "Your daughter is right here."

"This isn't the daughter I raised. The daughter I raised would know that staying overnight at a man's house can lead to her losing everything she's worked hard to protect. I pray to God you aren't so far gone that you've given up everything, but you're heading in that direction. You know you are. You're becoming just like Mari."

A flush of adrenaline rages through my veins. "And Mari's a bad person?"

His expression grows grim. "She's fallen away from the Lord, and it shows. Hector is like a brother to me, and she's breaking his heart. I just hope you don't break mine."

His condemnation of Mari for living like a regular college student is enough. I can't handle this anymore.

"Well, you should probably add me to your prayer list then. I don't plan on abstaining from sex anymore."

My dad's entire posture changes, his spine growing rigid. His hands drop to his sides. "I pray to God that isn't true." His voice is tight.

I huff out a humorless laugh. "I just told you it's true. Believe me."

My dad is utterly still. There's something strange about his expression as he stares steadily at me... His face crumples inward. He buries his head in his hands, and his shoulders start to shake rapidly. I stare at him for a moment, my head growing fuzzy.

The sound of his cry registers, and a chill runs down my spine. It's high pitched and strange. I've never really seen my dad cry. At most, I've seen him with red, teary eyes and a bit of a grimace. I've certainly never heard it.

When my daze clears, I snap into action. I rush over to him and wrap my arms around him. "It's okay, Dad. I'm still me."

"You were my little girl," he says, or I think he does. His voice is muffled through his sobs.

Under different circumstances, I might try to have a blunt discussion with him about how purity culture teaches men to infantilize their grown daughters, but I can't right now. Not while he's weeping.

Instead, I squeeze him tightly. "I still am. This has nothing to do with my relationship with you. You're still my hero, just like you were when I was little."

It's only a partial truth. Over the last year, my dad has become much more human than hero in my eyes, but right now, he needs my comfort.

"Dad." It's Vanessa's gentle voice. When I glance up, she's standing a few feet away, her brow furrowed. She hates seeing him like this as much as I do. "We love you more than anything, but we're becoming adults now. We have to figure out things for ourselves. That's what God wants for us, too."

"It happened too fast," he says. "This isn't how it's supposed to be."

Goodness, he sounds so young. I shoot my sister a sad smile, and she returns it. How strange that we're here comforting our father who once seemed like the king of the world. No one but God was bigger than him in our youth.

Hours later, I lie in my bed with my sister next to me. She asked to spend the night in my room, probably because she's worried about me after the turmoil of the day.

"Ness," I whisper, "Are you awake?"

"Yeah." Her voice is faint.

"What am I going to do if Cole begs to be in a relationship with me?"

She clears her throat. "Do you think that's what he's going to do?"

"I think so. He's desperate, but it's not what he really wants." I clench my jaw. "After we had sex, he said he still doesn't believe in monogamy. Clearly, it wasn't good enough for him to want to be with me long term. To want it *only* with me. Would you want a love like that? Would you want someone who's only in a relationship with you because it's a better alternative to losing your friendship?"

She's quiet for a moment, and the heaviness of the week pulls my body like a magnet into my bed.

"No," she eventually says. "I would only want to be with him if he were madly in love with me, especially if I loved him as much as you do."

My throat grows tight. "Exactly. That's exactly how I feel."

"But I wouldn't turn him down unless I knew for sure. It's hard for me to imagine anyone being this desperate to keep someone in their life if they weren't in love."

That's because you're not weak enough to let yourself become a person's only source of emotional comfort for five years straight while you wait for them to see you as something more.

I turn to my side and squeeze my eyes tightly shut. I can't think about this now. I'll wait until I hear what he has to say.

NINETEEN

Cole

I'M SOAKED with sweat by the time I make it inside my parents' house. As soon as I walk into the kitchen, I pour myself a glass of water and drain it. I don't think I've run a six-minute mile since I quit baseball.

Three days without her, and I waiver between despair and strange bursts of breathless euphoria, which might be the result of lack of sleep.

But it might not be.

Maybe I needed this. Maybe this hell I'm living in now is actually a wonderful gift. Without it, I might never have crawled out of my deep pit of denial.

Losing her friendship has opened the door to that beautiful world I got to live in for less than twenty-four hours. The one I was too terrified to make my permanent home.

"Honey," my mom says, pulling me out of my head. I've been spending a lot of time here with her since Livvy left. Even though I haven't been brave enough to share more than I did a few days ago, my mom's presence soothes me. "You have dark circles under your eyes. You're not sleeping."

"I'm not going to be able to sleep well until I talk to her."

Her brow knits. "And what if your talk doesn't go well?"

My throat constricts at the thought, but I push it away. "I can't think about that right now."

Her frown deepens. "You need to talk about what you're feeling. Holding it in doesn't do you any good."

"I'm too tired to talk."

She sighs. "Well, you know I'm here when you need me."

"Is that right?" a deep voice says.

When I glance up, my dad's tall form hovers in the kitchen entryway. He stands with his hands on his hips and a cynical smile on his face. "How can you be here for him if you're breaking up this family?"

Jesus, is he drinking? He looks worse than I did the last time I looked in a mirror, with his red face and puffy eyes. When I shoot a questioning look at my mom, she shakes her head slightly before looking back at my dad. "I'm breaking up with you, not my children. Oh, and by the way, I talked to Allen yesterday, and I have great news about the estate. I mean, when I say you'll be happy—"

"Allen." My dad's eyelids grow lazy. "So you're on a first-name basis with him already. That was quick."

I scowl. "Chill out, Dad. Most people are on a first-name basis with their lawyer. As you are, by the way, with all of the company lawyers. Leave her alone. You sound like a fucking child."

My mom frowns at me. "Don't talk to your dad like that."

I'm about to roll my eyes at her, but the look my dad's face freezes me. He's staring at my mom with an emotion I recognize well, because it's all I've felt these past several days.

It's longing.

He's probably thinking about how my mom won't be around to defend him after the divorce. She won't have his back, and anyone who's been blessed enough to have her loyalty knows what a loss that is.

My mom turns to him, and if she notices his look, she doesn't show it. "Anyway, *Allen*—" she raises her brows, "—has a whole plan about how we can keep the kids' trusts completely intact. I didn't fully understand it, but hopefully, once you hear it, you can break it down for me."

"I don't want to hear any of it," my dad says, and I can't keep myself from gawking at him. His petulance is strange to watch, like I'm seeing a version of him from decades ago, long before I ever knew him.

He rushes over to the fridge and pulls out a beer. I shoot a wide-eyed look at my mom, but she doesn't seem surprised.

"Mark, honey, you have the Vons meeting later..."

He ignores her and twists off the lid of his beer with his bare fist. "Don't call me 'honey'. You've given up that right."

My mom purses her lips. "Do you need me to text Lily and have her reschedule it for you?"

"I'm perfectly capable of texting her myself."

She turns to me and claps her hands together once. "Alright" Her voice is chipper. "I'm late for my knitting club, so I need to head out."

As she walks out of the kitchen, my dad follows her with his gaze. He's not even trying to hide his desolation.

Jesus, he looks so sad and....

Kind of pathetic.

It's unsettling, and it makes something soften inside my chest. I'm not affectionate with him anymore. Any affection I show is perfunctory, like a quick hug after coming home from a school break. It's so strange that I want to reach out and touch his shoulder and ask if he's doing okay.

I clear my throat. "Divorce is hard, Dad. It's well known that it's harder on men."

He lifts his beer and takes another big gulp. "We're not getting a divorce."

I avert my gaze, heat washing over my skin. Good God, this is really getting sad. He's falling apart. Meanwhile, my mom seems just fine.

"As long as you're drinking, are you sure you don't want something stronger?" I ask. "I've got a bottle of Johnny Walker Blue at the guesthouse. I was saving it for a rainy day, and I'm probably as miserable as you are."

He doesn't hesitate for a moment. "That sounds great."

A while later, my dad and I sit in my living room. He stares down at the brown liquid in his glass as he swirls it around. Having just run a hand through his hair, one side of it is slightly fluffed out.

Sophia said he was sad after he had sex with her. Maybe this is what she was talking about.

But why? Why would he pine for my mom when he's brazenly ignored her for years?

"You'll be okay, Dad. You know that, right?"

His gaze is fixed on his whiskey, and the only hint that he heard me is the slight tick of his jaw.

"You're a good-looking guy," I say. "You'll get married again. I've heard women my age say you're hot."

And I know for a fact that you've fucked women my age. Of course, but there's no reason to bring up Sophia.

"I don't want to marry a twenty-two-year-old girl. That's not a real wife."

I strain my eyes to keep them from rolling. He's in too much pain for me to be mean, but I guess a "real wife" is supposed to take care of him and every aspect of his life while he fucks twenty-two-year-old girls behind her back.

"Then you can find a nice forty or... How old are you?"

"I'm forty-eight." He frowns into his glass. "It's too much work. I won't ever get married again."

"We both know that's not true."

He lifts a hand and runs it through the other side of his hair, so now his whole head is disheveled. "Your mom's going to get remarried right away. Let's say a year. Do you want the over or under?"

Jesus, does he really think I'm going to make a bet like that about my own mother? "How drunk are you?"

"Not drunk enough."

"Do you even know Mom at all?"

He scowls. "It won't be hard for her. She never loved me."

Good God. What a melodramatic, self-serving view of their failed marriage. Do all men of his generation throw themselves pity parties when their wives finally grow weary enough of their bullshit to divorce them? Is this why divorce is so hard for them as a rule?

"So you're implying that you love her?"

"I've always loved her."

His answer comes so quickly, it makes irritation flare over my skin. I grit my teeth to fight the retort rising to my tongue. *What crock of shit.* "You had an interesting way of showing it."

"I know I was a terrible husband, but we haven't really been married. Not for a long time, at least."

"Maybe you didn't want to be, but you had a wife at home when you were fucking other women. And you have three kids who love her and didn't want to see her hurting."

He flinches. "I wish I hadn't been so careless. What I did on that trip to Arizona is one of my biggest regrets. You shouldn't have seen that."

My pulse pounds like a drum in my ears. "You shouldn't have done it."

When he shuts his eyes, I take a deep breath. There's no reason to rehash it all now. Their marriage is over. My mom is moving on.

"I suppose technically it was wrong." His voice is much softer. "No matter what we agreed on."

I jerk back, a prickle of foreboding running over my skin. "What are you talking about?"

He stands up and walks to my kitchen counter. When he picks up the bottle of whiskey, I open my mouth to tell him he's had enough, but then he starts talking. The tone of his voice sends a ripple of alarm through me.

"I never should have married her." The dreamy quality to his voice tells me he's talking to himself. "She was so young, and I knew she was still in love with him. But I thought there was plenty of time for her love to grow. I couldn't let her go. I practically bullied her into marrying me." He shakes his head slowly. "I guess I got what I deserved."

A cold shiver runs down my spine. "In love with who? And what do you mean you got what you deserved?"

He jerks back, his eyes growing focused. "I shouldn't be talking to you about this."

"No." My voice is hard. "You can't drop hints like that and expect me to let it go. You deserved what? Did mom have an affair?"

He clenches his teeth. "You need to talk to her about it. All I'm going to say is that our marriage has been over for sixteen years. I was done, at least, but your mom wanted to keep our family together. She chose to stay married for you kids."

"This is fucking insane!" I take both hands and run them through my hair, clinging tightly and sending tingles into my scalp. "Are you making this up to get sympathy?"

"No!" He scowls. "I neither want nor deserve your sympathy. She would have reconciled if I had initiated it, but I didn't. I couldn't forgive her, so I kept punishing her over and over again. I could see that it hurt her, and I liked it."

"Dad, that's so fucked up."

"I know."

"Who did she have an affair with?"

"Her ex-boyfriend." His faint smile doesn't reach his eyes. "Her high school sweetheart. I would kill him right now if I had the chance, even after sixteen years."

"Jesus Christ. I never even knew she had a boyfriend before you."

He scoffs. "Have you seen your mom? If I hadn't snatched her up, someone else would have, which is why I married her when I knew she wasn't ready."

My vision grows dazed, and I stare at the floor. How is it possible that I got everything wrong? I thought my mom was ignored and lonely. Fragile. I thought she was so close to breaking that I never wanted to burden her with anything, and it made me hate my dad.

Maybe the pall cast over my world and memories also clouded my perception of her. Maybe I didn't see her correctly.

I withdrew from both of them after that trip to Arizona.

I lost both of them.

"I always thought she was sad," I say. "I thought she was just waiting around, hoping you would stop treating her like shit, and that's why she wouldn't divorce you."

"She wanted me to stop, but she wasn't waiting. She wanted to stay married so that she could give you kids a stable childhood, and she didn't want you to know about any of this. She was furious with me after Arizona."

"Why didn't you stop cheating? Why did you punish her for sixteen years if you supposedly love her?"

"I don't know." He lowers his head to his hands and runs his fingers through his hair again. "I didn't think I had to stop. I never thought she would divorce me, and even though our relationship was shit, at least she was mine."

My body grows utterly still.

Oh my God.

Isn't that what I did with Livvy? I didn't have all of her, but what I had was mine alone. I desperately needed her, and that gave her a terrifying power over me. It made me selfish and greedy. I kept her entirely to myself for years, and that meant I never had to confront what it would mean if she explored a life without me. If she'd dated... If she'd gotten a boyfriend...

I would have lost my mind. I nearly did from just watching someone else press his lips against hers.

My denial would have ended much sooner if I'd stopped clinging to her like I might die if I ever let go. No wonder she said I wanted her to live small. I would have locked her in a dungeon if it meant I could keep her forever.

Fuck, I'm a bastard.

She deserves so much more than what I've given her these past five years. She deserves to overcome all her fears and live a wildly full life.

I have to let her, no matter how much it terrifies me.

"You were afraid," I say.

"What do you mean?"

"You didn't want to reconcile with her because you didn't want to risk what would happen if she did something like that again. You were protecting yourself."

He sighs. "Probably. It was torture finding out what she did."

"Yeah, but isn't this worse?"

He sighs. "This is hell."

It is hell, but it doesn't have to be. Not for me.

I know exactly what I'm going to do. I know exactly how I can show her how much I love her.

"What am I going to do without her?" my dad asks, and the pain in his voice pulls me out of my head.

Oh God, he doesn't have the consolation of hope like I do. His stupidity has lasted longer and been much more destructive. He doesn't have a prayer of winning my mom back after all he's done.

I can't even imagine his agony.

"Dad..."

"What?"

"Um..." I exhale as I try to find the right words. "I think I've been a little unfair to you. Over the years, I mean."

At first, his brow knits, but then his whole expression softens.

"Don't get me wrong, I'm still mad at you. You're a dick for all the things you've done."

"I know."

"Walking in on you having sex with another woman was traumatizing. Literally traumatizing. I can't even think about it without feeling like I'm going to have a panic attack."

His expression grows somber. "You have no idea how much I regret my carelessness—"

I lift a hand. "Let me finish. Mom made a mistake. It was a big one, but it's fucked up that you've punished her for sixteen years over it."

"I know."

"I just..." I meet his gaze. "I want you to know that I'll be here for you during this divorce. I know you probably have a lot of reason to think I wouldn't be, but I love you, and I don't like that you're in so much pain."

He looks away from me and nods jerkily. I know it's to hide the fact that his eyes are misting. Oh God, I don't think I could handle it if he cried. I already want to burst with a tenderness I haven't felt for him since I was a teenager.

"To be honest," I say, "I was dreading starting work and having you as my boss, but I'm kind of looking forward to it now. Maybe we can start getting lunch together or something."

His smile is almost boyish, and it makes something click into place in my chest. "We can start going to games again," he says. "I can get Dodger's season tickets."

"I'd love that."

LATER THAT EVENING, I walk into my mom's knitting room.

"Hey," I say.

"Hey." She keeps her gaze fixed on her deftly moving fingers as she twists the blue yarn around the silver needles.

"So...Dad told me some things today."

"Oh." It's a small, faint sound, but there's a wealth of meaning behind it. There's only one thing he could have told me, and she knows what it is.

"Yeah. He seemed like he was telling the truth, but I won't believe it until you confirm it."

She shuts her eyes, her face grimacing. "It's true."

My throat grows tight, and I take a deep breath through my nose. "That's okay, Mom. I mean... Not that you were apologizing, but..."

Her grimace grows. "Do you wish I'd told you?"

I swallow. "No. It's none of my business. I wish I hadn't made so many assumptions about your marriage. I wish I had just left it between you guys."

She nods slowly. "I thought I could shield you kids from all of it, but looking back, that seems naive. I probably should have divorced your dad years ago. It would have been healthier for you all in the long run."

My body tenses. "Stop making it all about us. Think about yourself for once."

When her gaze snaps up, I finally see the tears, and my heart jumps into my throat. "I'm sorry. I didn't mean to yell."

"It's okay, honey." Her pained expression softens, and she wipes under her eyes. "Do you want to finally learn how to knit? I could use the company."

"Not even a little bit, but I can hang out with you while you knit. I could also use the company."

When she smiles, I join her on the couch.

"Do you want to laugh?" I ask as I pull my phone from my pocket. "Last night at, like, three in the morning, I sent this completely unhinged text to Livvy, and it's so pathetic, even I laughed when I reread it this morning."

She glances down at her needles. "I won't find it funny."

"Oh, Mom, you underestimate me. I become a poet when I'm depressed. A really, really shitty one."

She glares at me, though her lips are twitching slightly. "If you want someone to laugh about your depression, you've come to the wrong place. Read the room better."

I grin. "We'll see. We'll see if your maternal instincts can withstand my masterpiece of patheticness. I think you're going to lose."

It turns out, I don't make her laugh when I read her the text, but I am able to talk to her about the mixture of fear and hope that compelled me to write it in the first place, and the lightness I feel afterward makes me wish I had done this sooner.

TWENTY

Livvy

WHEN I SPOT Cole through the shaded glass, I hesitate at the entrance. He's sitting in the back corner with his phone in his hand, looking so handsome in his blue button-up shirt that I want to throw myself into his arms.

Thank God, I chose a Starbucks. I couldn't have met him in a more intimate setting. It would have been too tempting to throw away everything I've worked hard for just because he's beautiful and I'm horny.

His head jerks up almost as soon as I walk through the door. His gaze moves from the top of my head to my feet, like he's taking in every detail.

He's missed me.

I've missed him, too.

Still, I promised myself I would be strong today. I give him only a small smile back.

"You look handsome," I say as I pull out the chair across from him. "I forgot you started work this week."

He glances down at his shirt. "I actually don't have to dress up this much unless I'm meeting with a client. This was all for you."

My smile grows. "I love you in blue."

"I know you do, and I'm not going to tell you how many different blue shirts I tried on. It would give you secondhand embarrassment."

I lift a brow. "You only have like four."

"Oh, but I went shopping for work clothes. I bought at least ten more blue shirts. I was preparing for battle, Olivia Grace."

When my smile fades, his brows draw together. "Sorry," he says. "That makes it sound like I want to fight you about everything, and the truth couldn't be further from that."

"It's okay. I know you were just teasing. I was more surprised at hearing you call me Olivia."

His shoulders relax, and he smiles again. My belly flutters. I've missed that smile.

"How is work?" I ask, not ready to dive into everything yet. "Is it okay being around your dad so much?"

"Actually, yes. We've kind of...reconciled, I guess."

"Oh, Cole, that's amazing."

When he shuts his eyes for a moment, my stomach plummets.

"What's wrong?" I ask.

He laughs softly and shakes his head. He stares at the wooden table for a moment before lifting his gaze to meet mine. "I love it when you say 'Oh, Cole'."

"Do I say it a lot?"

"No." His smile softens. "But I love it when you do."

The tenderness in his eyes makes my chest constrict, and I

glance down at my lap to collect myself. "I guess we should probably talk about everything."

He clears his throat, and out of the corner of my eye, I see him straighten his posture. "I have a story to tell you."

My head jerks up. "A story?"

His smile grows abashed. "I rehearsed it—*many* times—and it still doesn't sound like I want it to. I was hoping I could make it really good and sweep you off your feet."

I swallow to ease the tightness in my throat. "I don't need a good story. I need a true story."

"It is that, and you were there for most of it, so it's not a new story, but I hope it will give you some perspective on why I'm such an idiot."

I frown. "You're not an idiot."

"I am, but I don't think I'm a hopeless idiot." He leans forward. "Can I tell you why?"

Goodness, it's so strange talking to him like this. He's being so much more cautious with me than he usually is. "Sure."

He smiles warmly, and my body grows light.

"Five years ago, around the time we met, I was going through a pretty deep depression. I didn't know that's what it was at the time. I don't think I really even knew what depression was. Everything looked darker, even my memories. I knew I had been happy at one time, but it felt like that happiness was never real, like it was flimsy. And things that used to make me happy didn't anymore."

I nod. "That's pretty common with depression."

"I know. You told me that back then. You were the one who helped me figure out I was depressed. I withdrew from my parents after I caught my dad cheating, and I didn't realize how much it affected me. They were the only people I could talk to, like *really* talk to." He smiles faintly. "And I'm sure you've noticed I'm a pretty sensitive guy, so that was hard."

I'm about to speak when his gaze bores into mine, making me forget what I was going to say.

"Then I met you." His voice grows hushed. "Livvy, I'm not exaggerating when I say you were like an angel who rescued me. I always call you an angel, because that's what you really were to me. Everything changed after we became friends. The world started looking brighter. I was happy again."

When my eyes start gathering moisture, I avert my gaze from his. I'm startled by the warmth of his hand on mine.

"I started to rely on you for happiness. I felt like I couldn't be happy without you, and it made me greedy. I told myself I was protecting you and being a good friend, but really, I was keeping you all to myself, and that wasn't fair."

I inhale a shaky breath. "You were young."

"That's not an excuse. You were never greedy with me. You have plenty of other people you share your feelings with. I only had you, and I didn't want anyone else. I needed you more than you needed me, and that was scary."

I nod jerkily, not knowing what to say.

His gaze darkens. "I was also wildly attracted to you. I would have pursued you, but the more I got to know you, the more I realized how different you were because of your religion. I didn't really understand Christianity before. I thought it just meant going to church once a week and forgetting about it when it was over."

"That's how it is for some people."

"I know." His swallow is audible. "If that's all it was for you, I would have pursued you. I could have done that. I'm not a dogmatic atheist. I could've become a Christian if it was just about going to church with you."

I nod. "You were really thinking about it back then?"

"Not just thinking about it. I tried it. I went to church for a year when I went away to college."

My head grows fuzzy, and I stare at his face for a moment. His expression is completely earnest.

"Are you serious?" I ask.

"Yeah."

"For an entire year?"

"Well..." He smiles faintly. "I didn't go every Sunday, because sometimes I was too hungover. My pastor even called me out on it one time."

"*Your* pastor. You actually knew the pastor of the church?"

"I did." His smile grows. "Pastor Jeremy. I can't say I liked him all that much. I probably shouldn't say this about a pastor, but I thought he was kind of a dick."

An almost hysterical giggle bursts out of my chest. "Some pastors are. The position can attract people who like power, which is why I've been on the lookout for a more... I don't know...unassuming pastor, I guess. What denomination was it?"

"Um..." His brow knits. "What you are. Pentecostal."

My body grows weightless. Jesus, I can't believe he did all this. He went to church for year. He found one in my denomination. He knew his pastor.

All for me.

"Why did you go?" I ask, even though I already know.

"I was trying to become the type of guy you wanted, but ultimately, I realized I couldn't. It just wasn't for me, and I knew you would see right through me if I pretended like it was."

My throat grows so tight I can hardly speak. "Why didn't you tell me?"

He hesitates for a moment. "I was terrified of how disappointed you'd be if you knew I didn't like it, because it means so much to you."

My eyes prickle. "I guess I was pretty judgmental back then."

"No." His tone is firm. "I never felt judged by you. I didn't go to church because I had any fear you didn't accept me as I was. I just wanted to become what you needed. Because I loved you, Livvy. I love you now, and I'll love you forever. You were right that I put you on hold. I wanted you all to myself, because I was so scared of what would happen if I let you go, which is why there's only one way to make amends." He swallows. "I have to let you go now."

When my mouth falls open, he averts his gaze. "I hope it's not forever. If I had my way, it wouldn't be for very long at all, but this isn't about me."

"What do you mean?"

"I came here today to let you know that I'm on hold for you. Do whatever you need to do to break out of your shell. You told me you've lived small because of me, and I want to show you that I don't want that at all. I want you to live a full life, even if it scares me. If you need to make out with other guys and...sleep around and experiment with your sexuality..." He exhales an unsteady breath. "I mean, I'm not going to lie, I hate even thinking about it, but I'll understand if that's what you need to do. Obviously, I shouldn't be around for it, since I've proven that I have no chill. But I'll be waiting. I'll be on hold for you." His voice shakes. "I'll be on hold forever if I need to be. There's no one in the world for me but you."

My heart is so light and airy, it could carry me to the sky. I want to tell him I don't want any of that. That I love him too much to make him prove himself. But that would be going back to my old pattern of giving him whatever he wants the moment he wants it.

For five whole years, I've accepted whatever I could get from him, as if it were all I deserved. If we're going to have a prayer of making it long term, I have to change the old patterns now. I need to prove to him that I'm no longer his angel, ready to fly in and rescue him from even the slightest turmoil.

Or maybe I need to prove it to myself.

"I have a lot to think about," I say.

His eyes alight. "Does that mean... You think you might take me off hold eventually?"

The hope in his voice makes my heart flutter. "Did you think I wouldn't even consider it?"

He exhales an unsteady breath. "I don't know what I thought. I've been so scared that I fucked everything up for good." When he lifts up his hand and holds it in front of me, his fingers are shaking.

Jesus, give me strength. I don't want him to be this scared. Do I really need him to prove himself?

Yes.

I'm not submissive any longer, at least not outside of the bedroom. I can do this.

I can make my own demands.

"I don't really like the idea of keeping you on hold indefinitely," I say. "That would make me selfish."

He smiles warmly. "You deserve to be selfish for once."

I shake my head. "What if we use my impurity contract deadline? What if we decide to meet on September seventeenth, and we can talk again then?"

His swallow is audible. "You mean like...you'll give me a definite answer? A yes or no forever?"

When I nod, he inhales deeply and runs a hand through his hair. "Sure. Whatever you want. I'm not going to lie though, the thought of getting a no from you is terrifying." He laughs humorlessly. "I think I'd rather just live in blissful ignorance."

"But it's healthier for both of us if you don't."

His gaze grows unfocused as it roams the surface of the

table. "So we'll meet up again on September seventeenth, and you'll tell me how you feel?"

"That will be our deadline," I say. "If I come up with an answer for you before then, I'll come to you."

He releases an almost hysterical laugh. "Wow, you really want to torture me, don't you?"

I smile sadly. "No, I don't. What I want to do is give you everything you need to make you feel better, but I have to do what's best for me."

"I'm glad you're standing up for yourself."

He doesn't sound the least bit glad, and his expression grows so desolately melancholy that I want to set my hand on his arm like I usually do. I may always be this soft on the inside, but I don't have to let it guide my choices.

Not when my will is iron.

"WHY WOULD you wait until September seventeenth if you already know what you want right now?" Mari asks.

"I agree," Vanessa says, lifting both hands and brushing away the flyaway strands of hair blowing frantically over her heart-shaped face. "The date seems pointless now, like you're just trying to make Cole suffer."

I look away from both of them, not ready to talk about this just yet. It's been twenty-two days since I last saw Cole. Despite my vow to go out and have adventures, these have been some of the dullest weeks of my life—full of morning prayer walks and late-night journal sessions. We were invited out by Travis and a few friends, but I declined. I didn't want to give him any false hope.

After being with Cole, I realized how impossible it would be to start anything with Travis. There was no spark there, nothing that could ever come close to the inferno that engulfed me when Cole so much as looked at me.

The most partying I've done is drinking a bottle of wine with Mari, but instead of going out to the bars afterward, we lay on her bed and binged all the John Wick movies.

It turns out that dullness was what I needed. I don't need to face the fear of putting myself out there anymore.

That's no longer my biggest fear.

My purity ring is pinched between my fingers, and I press it firmly into the wet sand, leaving behind a circular imprint.

"Maybe I should bury it," I say.

Without seeing Mari's face, I know she's rolling her eyes at me. "Why don't you just keep it, since you obviously don't want to get rid of it?"

"Burying it is a happy medium. I can bury it now and come back in a couple of years and dig it up. I'll bring some of my old prayer journals and reflect on the person I used to be and how much I've changed. I'll toss it in the water then if I'm ready."

Mari's bare feet step into my view. "Do you know how sand works? You'll never find it again. If you want to be able to dig it up, you need to bury it in your backyard."

"Or don't do anything with it," Vanessa says. "Keep it in your tin box."

Mari plops down next to me. "I second that. It's clearly important to you, and why wouldn't it be? It shaped who you are, and I happen to adore who you are. I wouldn't change a thing about you."

"I wouldn't either, Livvy."

Mari sets her hand on my shoulder. "We don't get to go and pick and choose the parts of ourselves we want to keep. That's the shitty part about trauma. It'll always be with you, even when the pain of it is gone."

Small grains of sand scrape against my finger as I slip the

ring back on. "The sad thing is that I don't even see this ring as trauma. I know, in theory, those purity conferences were toxic, but looking back, they're happy memories. Do you feel that way too, Mari, or am I crazy?"

Her brow knits and her gaze grows unfocused. "I hardly even remember them."

I glance out at the water. "I guess I deal with trauma differently, because I'm getting warm and fuzzy just thinking about them. We'd take the First Covenant bus to LA with the whole youth group. We'd be in those big auditoriums with hundreds of other weirdo evangelical kids, which made me feel way more normal. When I look at it now..." I glance down at my ring. "I feel nostalgia."

Mari looks at me incredulously. "Which is a positive emotion."

"Yeah."

"So why do you want get rid of it?"

"Keep it for nostalgia's sake," Vanessa says. "Why bury it? Just put away somewhere and pull it out when you want to do some reflecting."

"I feel like the fact that I can't get rid of it means something ominous. I was able to burn my letter to my future husband. I was able to end my friendship with the man I love. Why can't I toss this ring?" I shake my head. "I think it's a sign that I'm not ready to change. If I take Cole off hold, I'm going to make him my whole world again. I'll make my needs secondary to his. Even if he's changing, I'm scared that I won't. I don't think he ever meant for me to be submissive to him. I did it all on my own. What if I do it again?"

Vanessa stares at me for a moment, her dark brows drawing together. "That's the dumbest fucking thing I've ever heard."

Mari's eyes grow wide. She looks away and drops her gaze to the sand, as if giving us privacy.

I pin my sister with a glare. "Excuse me?"

She softens her voice. "Why are you being so black and white about this when you've probably told me a million times in just the last month that you don't think in black and white anymore?"

An electrical current runs over my skin. Holy shit, she's right. How am I still doing this without even realizing it?

I guess black-and-white thinking is my default when I'm afraid.

"You're not deciding your whole future," Vanessa says. "You're not picking out who you're going to be for the rest of your life. You're choosing what you want right now, and you already know what you want."

My throat grows too tight to speak. I swallow to ease it away. "I do."

TWENTY-ONE

Cole

MY ARMS FEEL LEADEN as I stuff the last few shirts from my bottom drawer into the cardboard box. It makes no sense that I'm so worn out after two hours of packing.

I thought I would love moving out of the guesthouse, since I'm constantly surrounded with reminders of her here, but clearing it all out leaves me somehow even more miserable, and I didn't think it could be any worse.

This was home for a brief moment. The eighteen hours she spent in this house were the happiest of my life.

I may never feel that again.

There's a knock at the door, and my stomach jolts.

It's soft, just like her knock. But my mom's knock is soft, too. Not like Livvy's though. Oh God, I think it's her.

As I rush to the door, I try hard to manage my expectations. It's probably not her. I'm probably hearing things because I'm so desperate to see her.

When I open the door and find her beautiful smiling face, a dizziness settles over me. "It's July!"

"It is July." She smiles cheekily and looks to the side.

My pulse pounds like hammer against my throat. "Livvy, don't fuck with me. Why are you here?"

When her eyes widen, I flinch. Jesus, why am I practically yelling in her face when she might be here to tell me she wants to be with me? I shut my eyes and take a deep breath. "Sorry, you just surprised me."

She sets her soft hand on my arm, and I could die at the pleasure of it. "It's okay," she says. "I'll spare you the suspense. I'm taking you off hold. I want to be with you."

Everything grows heavy. The joyful misery that began five years ago has finally come to an end. I love her, and she's mine.

I grab her so quickly that she shrieks. Maybe I'm acting like a madman, but I couldn't stop myself if I tried. I lift her up high in the air and throw her over my shoulder.

"Oh my gosh," she shouts. "What are you doing?"

"I'm taking you to my bedroom."

She giggles. "I thought we were going to talk first."

"We can talk later. I caught you. You're mine now."

I toss her roughly onto the bed, pulling off her clothes as I crawl on top of her. She's grown bolder since the last time we did this, unzipping my jeans and pulling them off along with my boxers.

"Are you moving?" she asks as she cups my balls.

I hiss as I grab her face and kiss her frantically. "Yeah, tomorrow." I pull away and lower my head to her chest. "God, I've missed this." I suck on her nipple. "I've thought about nothing but this these last three weeks."

"Me too."

I trail my fingers up her thigh and slip one inside her pussy. "You're wet for me already. Good girl."

She releases a breathless laugh. "I can't believe this is happening so fast."

"Get used to it."

I press soft kisses along her neck, and she hums. "I will."

As soon as I get the condom on, I shove myself inside her. I can't do preliminaries. Not when I've been so starved for her. Not when I've spent the three weeks wondering if I would ever be in heaven again.

"I love you," I tell her as I thrust.

"I love you too."

I pull all the way out and ram back in. "Why did you take me off hold early?"

She whimpers. "I needed more of this."

I want to laugh, but instead, I make my body grow still. "No. Be a good girl and tell me the real reason."

She smiles faintly as she lifts her hand into the air and spreads her fingers apart. She pulls off the silver ring, grabs my hand, and drops it into my palm. "I wanted to give you this."

I close my hand around it. "You took me off hold to give me your purity ring?"

"I've been trying to get rid of it for weeks, and I haven't been able to. I finally realized why." Her smile fades. "I always imagined giving it to you."

I swallow. "You thought I'd be your husband someday."

Her nod is jerky. "I'm done with purity culture, but I'm not done with you. This is only the beginning for us."

My vision grows misty. "Oh fuck, Livvy." My voice trembles. "Are you real? Are you sure you're not an angel?"

She shoots me a sultry smile before lifting her head and biting down softly on my neck. "I hope not. I like being naughty too much."

I grin as I pull out of her and thrust back inside her tightness. Fuck, she's perfect.

"I'm never letting you go," I grit out. "You're never getting away from me."

She lifts her hips to meet mine. "I'm yours now."

The next several minutes are a fever dream, as if my body disappears into hers. She's the only thing I need. My fallen angel who's mine because I caught her.

AFTERWORD

Thank you for reading Cole and Livvy's story. I'm a new indie author and reviews are really helpful in getting exposure. If you enjoyed *Purity*, I'd greatly appreciate it if you went to Amazon or Goodreads and told the world what you think.

If you want more Purity content, go to skylermason.com and sign up for my monthly newsletter. Everyone on my email list will receive a spicy epilogue with a peek in Cole and Livvy's future.

Join my Facebook reader group:
Skyler Mason's Angsty Book Club

And follow me on social media here:
instagram.com/authorskymason
facebook.com/authorskymason
twitter.com/authorskymason

ALSO BY SKYLER MASON

ACKNOWLEDGMENTS

Gabrielle Sands, you rescued this book from disaster twice. You were my angel, the Livvy to my Cole (except I don't want to spank you).

My amazing editor Heidi Shoham, thank you for making the dialogue in this book so much snappier. Every time I apply your feedback, I become a better writer.

My PA Tiffany, thank you for keeping my lazy, disorganized self in check. My life would be a disaster without you.

My sensitivity reader Carla Peterson from Carla_is_reading, thank you for your thorough feedback on Mariana's character. I'm so excited for you to help me write her book!

My excellent proofreader Taylor West, thank you for making this book as polished as it can be and for your endless encouragement.

To my beautiful beta readers, Kasey, Jasmine, and Ellie, your support and feedback over the years has meant the world to me. You have no idea how much I appreciate you!

9 781088 028797